To Carly who Rebuilt me, I love
and mam – whatever will be, will be

First Edition

Chapter 1: A Not-So-Warm Addition

The squad room of the Washington station, part of Northumbria police Constabulary, nestled near The Galleries Shopping Centre, buzzed with its usual Monday morning energy. Officers huddled around their desks, cradling half-empty mugs of tea or coffee as conversations ebbed and flowed. The air was thick with the scent of cheap caffeine and bacon butties, mingled with the faint rustle of case files being shuffled.

At the front of the room stood Chief Superintendent Adams, a man whose presence seemed as permanent as the building itself. His broad frame and gruff expression were framed by a thick, grey moustache that twitched when he was displeased—which was most of the time. Today, he held a clipboard in hand, his eyes scanning the room like a hawk surveying its territory.

"Alright, listen up!" Adams's voice cut through the low hum of chatter like a cannon blast. His tone held the authority of a man who had seen it all, demanding attention. "Busy day ahead, and we need to get moving."

The chatter dulled instantly, and all eyes turned toward him. Adams wasted no time assigning cases, his voice a steady rhythm of authority. "Waters and Jones—burglary at an address in Concord. Check the footage, and don't stop off at Greggs for once."

A ripple of laughter rolled through the room, a momentary break in the tension. Waters and Jones exchanged knowing smirks as they stood to grab their coats, but Adams wasn't one for lingering humour.

"Peterson and Daniels—traffic incident on the A1 near the Angel. Lamp post versus car. Make sure it's just driver stupidity and nothing more."

Murmurs followed, and the shuffle of movement filled the air as the rest of the workload was allocated and the officers collected their files. But then, just as Adams reached the last name on his list, there was a brief, almost imperceptible pause. His eyes flickered with something—a hesitation, perhaps—before his gravelly voice called out again.

"Detective Grimshaw."

The name settled over the room like a cold wind. A ripple of whispers followed, soft but noticeable. The new detective had been the subject of station gossip for days. Some said he was brilliant, others described him as unsettling. Most agreed there was something about him that didn't quite sit right, though no one could put their finger on it.

Adams cleared his throat as if to dispel the unease. "Ah yes, our new detective." His gaze found Detective Mortimer Grimshaw, seated in the far corner of the room like a shadow.

Grimshaw rose to his feet, his movements deliberate and calm. His appearance, at first glance, was unremarkable. Pale skin neatly combed dark hair, and a well-tailored suit. Yet something about him—perhaps the stillness with which he carried himself or the cool detachment in his eyes—made the others uneasy. It was as if he existed on the edge of the room, observing rather than participating.

"Sir," Grimshaw responded, his voice low and steady. The conversations that had begun to pick up again stopped abruptly. There was something in that voice space controlled, precise, yet cold as winter.

Adams gave a curt nod, clearly choosing to ignore the tension. "Detective Grimshaw, I've heard good things about you. Let's get you settled." His tone was clipped, business-like, but even Adams couldn't entirely shake the undercurrent of uncertainty in the air.

There was no mention of the rumours that had been swirling like smoke around Grimshaw's arrival. No acknowledgement of the way the room seemed to quiet whenever he was mentioned. Adams didn't deal in rumours. He dealt with facts. And right now, the fact was that Grimshaw was part of the team, and with the report from his previous superintendent a damn good detective.

"And your partner today," Adams continued, scanning his clipboard, "will be Sergeant Harper."

At the back of the room, Sergeant Chloe Harper shot up from her seat, her mouse blonde hair catching the light as she moved. She beamed, her enthusiasm radiating across the room like a burst of sunlight. "Yes, Chief!" she replied, practically bouncing toward Grimshaw with the kind of energy that stood in sharp contrast to his stoic demeanour. A few officers exchanged relieved glances—they wouldn't be the ones paired with the new guy.

Harper stopped in front of Grimshaw, her grin wide and welcoming. "Hi! I'm Clo—nice to meet you!" She thrust her hand forward as if her cheerfulness alone could thaw the cold around him.

Grimshaw regarded her hand for a long moment, his face unreadable, before he extended his own. His grip was firm but unnervingly cold. Harper didn't seem to notice—or care. If anything, her smile grew wider.

"Right," Adams interrupted, clearing his throat and snapping the room back to attention. "You two are on a missing person case. A fourteen-year-old girl didn't come home after a sleepover. Family's panicking, so let's handle this quickly."

"Got it, Chief," Harper chirped, already turning back to Grimshaw. "We're on it."

With that, Adams dismissed the room with a wave of his hand, and the squad erupted into motion. Officers pulled on coats and headed out the door, but not without casting a few lingering glances at Grimshaw. His unsettling aura clung to him like a second skin—enough to make people curious, even wary, without knowing exactly why.

Harper, undeterred by the whispers or the odd glances, stayed at Grimshaw's side. "First day, huh?" she said, her tone bright as ever. "Must be a whirlwind. Welcome to the team."

Grimshaw nodded slightly, his face still impassive. "Thanks," he replied, his voice flat but not unfriendly. There was a pause, and for a brief moment, Harper seemed to consider how to break through his wall of reserve.

"You know," she began again, as they walked toward the door, "I've never partnered with someone on their first day. Fancy grabbing a coffee on the way? Might as well fuel up before we start."

Grimshaw's gaze flicked to her for a brief second, then back to the file in his hands. His voice was laced with the faintest trace of dry humour. "Sure. The darker, the better."

Harper let out a light and genuine laugh. "Alright, then. Dark it is. We'll get you sorted."

As they stepped out of the station and into the cool morning air, Harper glanced sideways at her new partner. There was something playful in her expression. "So, what's the secret to drinking the darkest coffee imaginable?"

Grimshaw remained stone-faced, his long strides matching her quicker pace. But as they approached the car, she could have sworn she saw the faintest hint of a smirk tugging at the corner of his mouth.

They climbed into the car, Harper sliding into the driver's seat. She fiddled with the radio for a moment before glancing over at Grimshaw. "So, a missing girl, huh?" she said, her tone growing more serious. "Do you think this one's a runaway or something worse?"

Grimshaw didn't answer immediately. He opened the file, his eyes scanning the details with cold precision. "Fourteen years old," he said quietly, more to himself than to her. "No history of running away. Close-knit family, at least on paper."

Harper raised an eyebrow, waiting for more. "So...?"

"So," Grimshaw continued, closing the file and turning his gaze out the window, "it's too early to tell. But if she hasn't come home by now, we should prepare for the possibility that this isn't just a case of teenage rebellion."

His words hung in the air, and Harper felt a chill creep down her spine. It wasn't what he said—it was how he said it. Calm. Controlled. As if he had already seen where this was heading and didn't particularly like the destination.

"You've done this before, haven't you?" Harper asked, her voice softening as she steered the car onto the main road.

Grimshaw didn't look at her, but his voice, when it came, was distant. "More times than I care to count."

The car fell into silence after that, the weight of the case settling between them. Harper wasn't one to let tension sit for too long, though. After a few minutes, she shot Grimshaw another sideways glance. "Well, let's hope we're wrong about this one. And in the meantime, I'll make sure you get that dark coffee."

Grimshaw finally turned to look at her, his expression as unreadable as ever, but there was something in his eyes—a flicker of appreciation, perhaps. "I'll hold you to that."

Harper grinned and hit the accelerator, the car speeding along the Washington highway towards the family home of the missing girl. The day had only just begun, but already it felt like the shadows were gathering.

As they drove, Harper's mind flickered back to the whispers she'd heard about Grimshaw—the quiet speculations and unspoken fears. There was more to him than met the eye, that much was clear. But whether he was a man burdened by ghosts or simply a man shaped by them, only time would tell.

For now, there was a missing girl to find, and somewhere in the back of Harper's mind, a nagging feeling told her that this case—this partnership—would lead them both into uncharted territory.

Chapter 2: Shadows of the Family

As they turned right at the roundabout signposted Houghton-le-spring Chloe asked, "Hope you don't mind me driving?", her voice teasing, though her eyes betrayed a growing seriousness. There was something about missing person cases that always hit close to home, something about the thought of a child alone in the world.

Grimshaw glanced at her, his face as unreadable as ever. "You will need to" he replied, his tone flat.

Clo raised an eyebrow, curiosity slipping into her expression. "Why? Something wrong with yours?"

Grimshaw's response was quick, still neutral but with a slight edge. "Don't have one."

Surprise flickered across Clo's face. "You don't have a car?" She half looked at him

There was a pause, barely noticeable, but enough to suggest Grimshaw wasn't eager to elaborate. "Let's just say I had a few… issues in my last role. Means you don't need a car when you don't have a licence".

Clo blinked, clearly intrigued, but sensing this wasn't a topic he wanted to dive into—at least not yet. She pressed her lips into a playful smile. "Issues?" she echoed with a hint of amusement before letting the subject drop. "Well, you're in luck. I'm an excellent driver."

"I guess this means I'll be chauffeuring you around from now on," Clo remarked, her fingers drumming lightly against the steering wheel as they pulled out of the lot.

Grimshaw glanced sideways at her, the barest twitch of his lips suggesting a smile. "Seems that way."

The light banter faded as they drove closer towards Houghton-le-Spring. The grey rooftops of the town loomed ahead, and with them came the quiet realisation of what lay in store. The conversation shifted naturally as the Reid residence came into view—a neighbourhood where everything appeared unnervingly perfect. Manicured lawns, freshly painted fences, flowers arranged just so. It was the kind of place where no one wanted to acknowledge the cracks beneath the surface.

"We're here to bring Molly home," Clo said, her voice quieter now, the playfulness gone. There was a determination there, tempered by the gravity of the situation.

Grimshaw nodded, his expression as unreadable as ever, though his silence spoke volumes. They pulled into the driveway, stepping out into the cool air that wrapped around them like a shroud. Clo gave Grim a sidelong glance, her usual brightness dimmed by the weight of the moment. "Ready?"

Another curt nod from Grimshaw, his face still a mask of detachment. They approached the Reid's' front door with purposeful steps, Clo's knuckles rapping softly but firmly. A moment passed, and then the door opened to reveal Mrs Reid, pale and trembling, her eyes red and swollen from crying. She looked fragile as if the slightest wrong move might shatter her completely.

"Mrs. Reid?" Clo said, her voice gentle but authoritative. "I'm Sergeant Harper, and this is Detective Inspector Grim. We're here to help bring Molly home."

At the mention of her daughter's name, Mrs. Reid's eyes filled with fresh tears. Her lips trembled as she stepped aside, nodding mutely for them to enter.

The house was unnervingly pristine. Everything in its place, every surface spotless. The stark white walls gave it a cold, almost sterile feeling, like a house that had been polished to mask the chaos hiding underneath. Family photos hung in neat rows along the hall, and Grimshaw's sharp eyes quickly found Molly's face smiling out from several frames. But even in those smiles, there was something too rehearsed, too controlled—like a doll posed perfectly for display.

They were led into the living room, where Mr. Reid sat stiffly in an armchair, gripping a coffee mug so tightly that his knuckles were white. His face was a blank mask, but his eyes flickered with something—a tension, an emotion too fleeting to pinpoint. Grimshaw took it in, quietly cataloguing the details. He was good at noticing the things that went unsaid.

"Paul," Mrs. Reid's voice broke the silence, shaky and trembling. "The police are here to talk… about Molly."

Grimshaw stepped forward, his tone professional, but cool. "Mr. Reid. Detective Inspector Grim. This is Sergeant Harper. We'd like to ask you a few questions about Molly."

Mr Reid nodded curtly but said nothing. His eyes flicked to Grimshaw's, and for the briefest of moments, their gazes locked. Grim felt it then—that subtle but unmistakable undercurrent. Something hidden. Something unsettling.

Clo, always the empathetic one, took the lead. "We know this is a difficult time," she said softly, her voice warm and calming, "but we need to understand Molly a little better. Did she mention anything recently? A boyfriend, maybe? Anything that could explain why she's missing?"

Mrs Reid shook her head quickly, tears still brimming in her eyes. "No… no boyfriend. Molly's always been… different. She's into her music—gothic things, heavy metal. She's always kept to herself." Her voice broke, the weight of emotion slipping through. "She's just… special." Clo thought to herself "Sounds like she is the polar opposite of what the house portrays, could it just be teenage rebellion"

Grimshaw's gaze slid to Mr Reid, whose face twitched slightly at the mention of Molly's "gothic" style. There was a tension in that moment, something unspoken. Discomfort, perhaps. Disapproval. Grimshaw's instincts flared, though he kept his expression neutral. Whatever it was, it was there—just below the surface.

Clo caught Grimshaw's glance, the silent communication between them speaking volumes. They didn't need to voice it—they both sensed that something was off.

"Would it be alright if we took a look at Molly's room?" Clo asked gently. "It might help us get a better sense of things."

Mrs Reid nodded eagerly, relief flashing in her eyes. "Of course. It's just upstairs."

As Mrs. Reid led them up the stairs, Grimshaw glanced back at Mr. Reid, who remained seated, his silence growing louder by the second. There was something about the man's stillness, something about the way he seemed so detached from the conversation. Grimshaw felt it like a weight in the air—the things left unsaid.

Molly's room was a stark contrast to the rest of the house. Where the downstairs was all neat and polished perfection, Molly's room was shadowed and brooding. Posters of dark, heavy metal bands covered the walls—singers with wild hair and harsh voices that screamed rebellion. The curtains were thick, blocking out most of the daylight. But amidst the darkness, there were signs of something else. Her desk was a mess of contradictions—brightly coloured notebooks, pastel pens, and a poster of a pop star peeking out from under a stack of schoolbooks. It was as if Molly had been living in two worlds, pulled in opposite directions.

Clo moved around the room slowly putting on a pair of blue neoprene gloves while Grim pulled on a black pair, Chloe noticed this out of the corner of her eye but didn't remark, she went back to scanning the room, her eyes flicking between the band posters and the cheerful school supplies. "It looks like she was stuck between two worlds," she murmured, running a hand lightly over the notebooks. "But you can tell which one she preferred."

Grimshaw nodded, his eyes scanning the room with quiet intensity. "This room leans heavily toward the darker side."

Something caught Grimshaw's eye at that moment, a small glint of metal beneath a pile of notebooks. He reached down a gloved hand, pulling out a sleek phone. The screen lit up, showing several missed calls—all from Mrs Reid. None from her father. The phone had been left behind, its notifications silenced.

"She didn't take her phone," Grim said, frowning as he handed it to Clo.

Clo glanced at the missed calls, her frown deepening. "Missed calls from her mum, but nothing from her dad." She turned the phone over in her hands. "Why leave it behind when you're going to a friend's sleepover? you take your phone. It's your lifeline. Unless running away was premeditated"

"Unless you don't want to be found," Grimshaw murmured.

He slipped the phone into an evidence bag and continued scanning the room. His eyes fell on a small, locked diary poking out from beneath a stack of notebooks. He picked it up, turning it over in his hands. "Locked," he muttered, his fingers already rifling through the desk drawers until he found a small key in a purse covered with band logos.

He handed both the diary and key to Clo. "You take a look. Teenage girls' journals aren't my territory."

Clo unlocked the diary with a smile and began flipping through its pages, her expression growing more serious with each entry. "Listen to this," she said softly. "'Everyone at school is the same. They all dress the same and act the same. I'm not like them. I wonder if things would be different if I was... normal like the other girls.'"

Grimshaw remained silent, though a flicker of something—understanding, perhaps—crossed his face.

Clo's voice grew sombre as she read on. "'He always says he wants me to be more like the other girls. More like them.'"

Grimshaw stiffened slightly at the word "HE." His thoughts immediately jumped to Mr. Reid—the tension in his silence, the way he hadn't called Molly even once. "HE," Grimshaw repeated softly. The pressure wasn't just coming from Molly's peers—it was coming from home.

"She's struggling with her identity," Clo murmured, flipping through more pages. "Trying to live up to what they want her to be. While trying to stay true to herself"

Grimshaw's voice was dark, quiet. "It's not just her friends. Her family's pushing her too. She doesn't feel like she belongs anywhere."

After sealing both the phone and the diary in evidence bags, Grim and Clo headed downstairs. Mrs Reid sat on the edge of the sofa; her worry etched into every line of her face. Mr. Reid remained in his chair, silent and unmoving, as though untouched by the weight of what was happening.

Clo held up the phone. "We found a phone in her room. Do you know if this belongs to Molly?"

Mrs Reid's eyes widened, and she nodded quickly. "Yes, that's hers. She never goes anywhere without it. Why didn't she take it?"

Her voice trembled with rising panic. "Why didn't she take it?"

Grimshaw's gaze flicked to Mr. Reid, but the man offered no explanation, no comfort. He simply sat, his silence becoming heavier with every second. Clo glanced at him as well, expecting something—anything—but his stillness remained.

"We also found Molly's diary," Clo said carefully, her voice steady. "We'd like to take it as part of the investigation. It might help us understand what she's been going through."

Mrs Reid nodded, but Mr Reid's voice suddenly cut through the room, sharp and cold. "No. That's private. She wouldn't want anyone reading it."

Both detectives paused, exchanging a glance. His objection was sudden—strange. Clo turned back to Mrs. Reid; her voice soft but firm. "If it helps bring Molly home, we need to take it."

The tension in the room was suffocating. Mr. Reid's silence stretched on, but it was clear that it was something that he wanted to keep hidden.

Grimshaw broke the silence, his tone calm but firm. "We need to review it. If it helps us find Molly, it's surely worth it. Don't you think so Mr Reid?"

Mr Reid slowly nodded in agreement.

Back in the car, Clo started the engine but didn't pull away. The silence between them was thick with unspoken thoughts. Grimshaw stared out of the window, his fingers tapping lightly against the door as he processed everything.

Finally, he spoke. "What did you make of it all?"

Clo exhaled slowly. "The mother's falling apart. She's terrified. But the father... he barely said a word, until we mentioned the diary, he got defensive. Something feels off."

Grimshaw nodded, his mind working through the puzzle. "Also, he didn't call her. Not once. Why wouldn't he call his missing daughter?"

Clo's hands gripped the steering wheel. "Yeah, I noticed that too. It doesn't sit right."

Grimshaw's voice softened, more reflective. "I know what it's like to be pressured into being something you're not."

Clo glanced at him, her curiosity building. "You think Molly's feeling that pressure?"

"Yeah," Grimshaw replied quietly. "Her friends, her family… they all want her to be someone she's not."

Clo gave him a small, determined smile. "We'll show her it's okay to be herself. We'll bring her home."

Trying to lighten the mood, Clo glanced over at Grim. "Alright. How about that coffee?"

As they pulled away, the weight of the case lingered between them. But beneath it all was a shared determination—to find Molly and to bring her back.

Chapter 3: Pieces of a Puzzle

The engine purred quietly as Clo and Grimshaw left the Reid's' house, the weight of their conversation still heavy in the air. Outside, the grey clouds above mirrored the mood between them, thick and unmoving, threatening rain but not yet delivering. Neither of them spoke, their silence heavy with reflection as the car carried them toward their next destination—a nearby industrial on the way to Molly's friend's house where the sleepover had taken place. The rhythmic clank of machinery drifted through the open windows, adding a mechanical hum to the quiet.

Clo pulled the car into a parking space near a small mobile coffee van parked beside a fire station. She stretched as she stepped out of the car, breathing in the cool air. "This is exactly what I needed. Fresh air and caffeine," she said with a grin, nodding toward the van. "Come on, let's grab a drink."

Grimshaw followed her, his long strides purposeful but silent. His hands were shoved deep into the pockets of his coat, and his expression remained thoughtful. The industrial park, with its wide grey expanse and steady noise of trucks and cranes, felt oddly peaceful. Clo approached the coffee van, ordering two coffees and inspecting the dark brew before handing one to Grim.

"Hopefully dark enough for you," she said with a grin, passing him the cup.

They wandered over to a weathered metal bench just along from the van, the distant whir of machinery punctuating the quiet between them. Clo took a sip of her coffee, the warmth providing some comfort against the chill in the air. She gazed out across the rows of grey warehouses and past the fire station, her mind still turning over the details of the case.

"So… who do you think HE is that she talks about in the diary?" Clo finally asked, her voice cutting through the hum of machinery.

Grimshaw didn't answer immediately. His gaze remained fixed on the skyline, the heavy clouds overhead mirroring the tangled complexity of the case. When he spoke, his voice was low, carefully measured, as though he were piecing his thoughts together as he spoke. "Everything suggests her father but without solid evidence it's hard to say for certain, but my gut tells me it is her dad which would lead to feeling trapped," he said. "Between the pressure from her father and the disconnect with her friends… it's enough to make anyone feel lost." He turned slightly, his sharp eyes meeting Clo's. "People like Molly… they look for a way out. Sometimes that means running and sometimes it could mean…" he left the sentence hanging but Clo knew what he meant as that thought had crossed her mind as well.

Clo nodded, her fingers tapping lightly against her coffee cup. "So do you think her dad's the reason she's gone?"

Grimshaw considered her question, his eyes narrowing as he thought back to the interactions with Mr. Reid. "He's definitely part of it," he said. "He's pushing her to be something she's not. It was written all over his face, and the diary confirmed it. He's got this idea of who Molly should be, and he won't accept anything outside that. Take a look at the contrast from the whole house it looked more like a show house than a family home, then you look at Molly's room and it's the total opposite"

Clo exhaled slowly, her breath creating a small mist in the cool air. "And what about the comment about everyone at school being the same?"

Grimshaw nodded, his gaze drifting back to the industrial park. "She's isolated. Not just from her father, but from everyone who should care about her. When you're that alone, you start looking for ways to disappear."

Clo studied him for a moment, a question forming in her mind. "You ever feel like that? Like you didn't fit in?"

Grimshaw's face remained impassive, but there was a flicker of something—perhaps a memory—behind his eyes. He took a long sip of his coffee before speaking. "Everyone feels it at some point," he said, his voice quieter now. "But yeah… I know what it's like."

A silence settled between them, thick with unspoken understanding. Clo was the first to break it. She glanced down at Grimshaw's coffee and smiled. "Dark enough for you?"

Grimshaw raised an eyebrow, and for the briefest of moments, a small smile tugged at the corner of his lips. "It'll do."

They sat there for a moment longer, as they finished their coffees in companionable silence. Clo stretched her arms over her head as they finally stood. "Ready to meet the friend?" she asked her tone light but determined.

Grimshaw nodded, his coat billowing slightly as they walked back to the car. The shift in the air was subtle but noticeable—the tension was still present but no longer suffocating. They drove in silence toward Sarah's house, Molly's friend, and the last person known to have seen her.

As they pulled up outside Sarah's house, the proximity to Molly's home struck them. Just three streets away, so close that Molly could have easily walked home. Clo parked the car and glanced over at Grim. "They lived so close," she mused. "It doesn't make sense that Molly didn't make it home."

Grimshaw's sharp eyes scanned the neat, orderly houses that lined the street. "Close enough to see each other every day. But distant enough to have separate lives"

They stepped out of the car and walked toward the front door of the well-kept house. A moment passed after they rang the bell and the door swung open to reveal a young girl about the same age as Molly, "this must be Sarah" thought Grim, dressed in pastel colours, her blonde hair perfectly styled. The contrast between her appearance and Molly's darker, more alternative look was stark. Both detectives noticed it immediately.

Grimshaw's face remained unreadable as he introduced himself. "Good afternoon. I'm Detective Inspector Grimshaw, and this is Sergeant Harper. We'd like to speak to Sarah."

Sarah blinked, momentarily thrown off by Grimshaw's demeanour. "That's… me," she said, shifting uncomfortably. "Is this about Molly?"

Clo stepped forward with a reassuring smile. "Yes. We understand she stayed here the night before last. We're just trying to get a clearer picture of what happened."

Sarah hesitated, her eyes flicking between Clo and Grimshaw, clearly nervous. "Yeah… come in." She stepped aside, allowing them into the brightly lit, neatly decorated home. The difference between this place and Molly's home was only slight but this had a warm family feel to it.

Clo asked, "Are your parents' home?"

"My mam is" replied Sarah

The three of them sat down in the living room, and a couple of seconds later they were joined by Sarah's mam, after introducing them both Clo began gently. "How long have you and Molly been friends?"

Sarah looked down at her hands, her fingers fidgeting as she spoke. "Since nursery. We've known each other forever." She hesitated, then added, "But we've… drifted apart recently."

Clo nodded; her tone soft but encouraging. "It sounds like you were close. Did anything seem different about Molly recently? Any changes in her behaviour?"

Sarah bit her lip, clearly unsure of what to say. "I don't know. She didn't talk about anything specific, but she's been quieter lately. More than usual. At school, we don't really hang out anymore. I've got my group, and she's... well, she's into different things."

Grimshaw tilted his head slightly, his voice probing but calm. "Different how?"

Sarah shrugged, her fingers twisting together in her lap. "She's into her music—the darker stuff. I'm into cheerleading, makeup, you know... the usual teenage girl things. We don't connect like we used to."

Grimshaw's expression remained impassive. "Can you talk to us about the sleepover?"

Sarah fidgeted again, looking uncomfortable. "Well... I didn't actually invite Molly at first. I didn't think she'd be interested. It's not really her thing."

Clo raised an eyebrow. "So how did she end up coming?"

Sarah sighed, guilt flickering across her face. "Our dads play golf together. Mr. Reid's always telling my dad how he wishes Molly was more like me. More outgoing. So, my dad suggested I invite her. He thought it would help."

Grimshaw's voice was calm but pressing. "Did it?"

Sarah shook her head, her blonde curls bouncing slightly. "Not really. Molly was quiet the whole night. She didn't talk much when we were discussing boys or music. She just sat there... not really part of it."

Sarah frowned, her brow furrowing in thought. "She just sat and played on her phone, but it wasn't her usual phone. Molly always had an iPhone, but this time it was an Android. I noticed because the notification sound was different. I just assumed that ~~he~~ she had a new phone and didn't think any more of it really."

Clo and Grimshaw exchanged a glance, their expressions sharpening. "Anything else unusual?" Clo asked gently.

Sarah bit her lip, her discomfort growing. "Molly didn't stay for breakfast the next morning. She left early. Gave me a hug, but it felt... off. Like she just wanted to get out of here."

Clo kept her tone calm but pressing. "Did she say anything when she left?"

Sarah looked down, wringing her hands together. "No... she just said goodbye and left. I didn't think anything of it at the time."

Grimshaw's expression darkened. "And you just let her go?"

Sarah winced at the sharpness in his tone, guilt creeping into her voice. "Well yeah, as I said we have been drifting apart and it just didn't seem like a big deal."

Back in the car, the air between Clo and Grimshaw felt heavier, the puzzle pieces slowly starting to fit together. Clo started the engine but didn't drive off right away. She sat there, thinking, her fingers tapping lightly on the steering wheel.

"The phone... that's significant, right?" Clo asked.

Grimshaw nodded, his voice thoughtful. "Very. If she had left her phone at home where was this other phone from?"

Grimshaw's eyes remained fixed on the road ahead, his expression unreadable. "There's more going on here than we've seen. The phone, her leaving early, the tension with her dad... we're missing something."

Clo's voice grew more determined. "We'll figure it out, we have to for Molly's sake"

Grimshaw turned to her, his face steady but with a flicker of resolve. "Yeah, we will."

The road ahead stretched out before them, full of unanswered questions, but they both felt the momentum of the case pulling them closer to the truth and more worryingly down a darker path. As they drove, the tension between them shifted. Clo glanced at Grimshaw, a small smile playing on her lips. "Alright. Time for more coffee?"

Grimshaw's face remained stoic, but there was a hint of humour in his voice. "Sure. The darker, the better."

Clo laughed softly as they drove away, the tension of the case still looming but with a growing sense that the pieces of the puzzle were finally starting to fall into place.

Chapter 4: The Echo of Isolation

The sun was sinking low, casting long shadows across the quiet suburban street as Grimshaw and Clo left Sarah's house. A fading light washed over the neighbourhood, but instead of bringing warmth, it seemed to deepen the sense of unease that lingered between them. The conversation they'd just had with Sarah echoed in their minds, leaving them with more questions than answers. As they drove Clo started to reflect on the conversation with Sarah.

"Well, that was… interesting," Clo finally said, exhaling sharply. "Molly was so out of place at that sleepover. Sarah didn't seem to notice—or maybe she didn't care."

Grimshaw's eyes remained fixed on the passing houses, his expression unreadable. "She was isolated. Disconnected. While they talked about *usual teenage girl stuff*, Molly didn't join in and just sat playing on her phone. That kind of separation isn't just physical—it's emotional and psychological. Molly was there, but not really there."

Clo nodded, replaying Sarah's recounting of the night. "It's like she was present, but only in body. Sarah said Molly didn't even stay for breakfast. She just left without a word. And that hug Sarah described— 'empty,' Like Molly was already gone and just did it out of habit. Also, I think it's clear that the HE she talked about in her diary was her father"

Grimshaw's voice was reflective but tinged with something heavier. "It's not just about belonging—it's about identity. Molly was being pushed into a Mold [mould]. By her father and by her peers. They wanted her to be 'normal,' to fit the same template as Sarah and her friends. But Molly wasn't like them. That kind of pressure, especially from a parent, eats away at you. It creates doubt, frustration, and resentment. It makes you feel like you're not good enough."

Clo tightened her grip on the wheel, her jaw clenching as she absorbed Grim's words. "And when your closest friend doesn't notice you're struggling? That makes it worse. Molly probably felt invisible." She paused, her mind turning to the most puzzling detail.

Grim's frown deepened. "Maybe she was keeping certain conversations off the radar. Away from her parents?"

The car hummed along the nearly empty road, the growing darkness outside mirroring the sense of isolation that had begun to close in around the case. Molly wasn't just missing—she had been lost long before anyone noticed.

Clo's voice softened, her empathy clear. "It's like being stuck in a room full of mirrors, but the reflection you see isn't who you are. It's who everyone else wants you to be. No wonder she left early. That sleepover could've been the last straw."

Grimshaw's gaze remained fixed on the road ahead, his voice gaining a personal edge. "I know what that feels like. That sense of isolation. Being the odd one out, surrounded by people who constantly remind you of what you're not."

Clo glanced over at him, curiosity flickering in her eyes. "You sound like you're speaking from experience." ← (he just said that)

Grim hesitated, his face unreadable, but the weight of his words hung in the air. "Maybe I am."

A moment passed between them; the silence heavy but shared—an unspoken connection. Both of them, in different ways, understood what it was like to be alone even in a crowd. Clo didn't push for more. She knew that some things didn't need to be said aloud.

The road stretched ahead, the sky now fully dark, as they continued toward the station. The hum of the engine filled the space between them until Clo broke the silence again. "Sarah described Molly's usual look—black hoodie, ripped jeans, combat boots. She was wearing her identity on the outside, saying 'I don't belong here.'"

Grim nodded, his expression thoughtful. "Her clothes were her armour. It's a way of protecting yourself, but also a way of keeping others at bay. Her music, her style—it was all about maintaining distance from people like Sarah."

"And Sarah didn't really know her, did she, well not any more?" Clo's voice was quiet, almost sad."

Grimshaw's voice grew darker. "Molly was struggling, and if she had anyone to confide in, Sarah wasn't aware of it. Sarah was supposed to be her closest friend, but she didn't even know what was going on."

As they pulled into the station's car park, the urgency of Molly's disappearance pressed heavily on them. It had been over 36 hours since she was last seen, and with each passing minute, the trail was growing colder. They needed something—anything—concrete to follow.

Inside the office, Grim's gaze shifted to the small diary they had found in Molly's room. "If she was hiding things, the second phone is just part of it. She might have written something in her diary. Maybe that's where we'll find a clue."

Clo nodded, picking up the diary. The worn cover felt rough under her fingers as she flipped through the pages. At first, it was filled with typical teenage frustrations—complaints about school and frustration with her father's overbearing nature. But deeper into the journal, something more significant appeared.

"There's something here," Clo said softly, pausing on a page that looked hastily written. She read aloud, cautious but intrigued. "'Met someone new online. They really seem to get me. Finally, someone who understands.'"

She looked up at Grim, her eyebrows raised. "This could be promising."

Grimshaw leaned in slightly, his expression hardening with focus. "She's talking about this new person like they're a lifeline. This is the first sign we've seen that she felt truly understood by someone."

Clo nodded, flipping through more pages. "But she doesn't give a name. No details about who this person is. Just that they listen. They don't judge her."

She turned the page, hoping for more, but the mention of this new friend abruptly ended. "It's frustrating—no clues about how they met or where this relationship was going."

Grim straightened up, his gaze distant as he pieced together the puzzle. "Maybe Molly was protecting them. Or maybe… she wasn't ready to admit how much this person was influencing her."

Clo closed the diary gently, her fingers tracing the cover. "Whoever this person is, Molly felt a connection. If they were online, it makes sense that she didn't want to write down too much—maybe to keep them a secret."

Grim glanced at the clock, his voice steady but urgent. "This is our best lead. We need to find out who this 'new friend' is. If Molly trusted them enough to mention them in her diary, they were important."

Clo nodded, her movements growing more purposeful. "Let's get into her phone. Digital Forensics set us up with a direct link to her accounts. We don't have to touch the device itself—we can go through everything right here."

Most of what she found were missed calls from Molly's mother—desperate attempts to reach her daughter. But one thing was glaringly absent.

"No calls or texts from her dad," Clo muttered, frowning as she continued scrolling through the call log. "Why didn't he try to call her, Grim? If your daughter's missing, wouldn't you try everything?"

Grimshaw's jaw tightened, his arms crossed as he stood over the desk. "Maybe he didn't think she'd answer."

Clo's brow furrowed as she considered the possibilities. "There's nothing unusual in the texts either. Just a few exchanges with Sarah about walking to school and some back-and-forth with her mum."

Grim's eyes narrowed, his voice low and sharp. "One thing stands out—no communication from her dad, even before she went missing."

Grimshaw stood back as Clo continued accessing the data. His mind raced through the possibilities—this new connection could be key, but it also raised new concerns. Who was this person? And why had Molly kept them hidden? More importantly, had they played a role in her disappearance?

The weight of the unanswered questions pressed heavily on both detectives as they worked late into the night, chasing the echo of isolation that Molly had left behind. But also a growing feeling of unease crept up the back of his neck, this felt familiar.

Chapter 5: DarkSeraphim

Grimshaw glanced at the clock on the wall, the ticking sound growing louder in his mind as time slipped away. Every second felt like sand running through his fingers, the chances of finding Molly dwindling with each passing moment.

It felt invasive, even wrong, to be digging through the most personal parts of Molly's life. But it was their only hope. If there were any clues, they were hidden somewhere in the messages, the photos, the conversations Molly had kept secret.

Grimshaw stood behind Clo, his tall frame casting a shadow over the desk. "Can you access her social media?" he suggested, his voice steady.

Clo nodded, her fingers already moving across the keyboard. "Instagram first." She paused for a moment, glancing up at Grim. "If the person she talked about in her diary contacted her online aye that's where they go in touch" [get]

Clo pulled up Molly's Instagram profile: GothGirl2010. The page was a digital reflection of everything they'd already seen in Molly's room—the dark aesthetic, the moody pictures, the heavy band logos that covered the walls. Selfies of Molly dominated the feed, showing her in full gothic attire. There were pictures of her dressed in black hoodies, combat boots, and ripped jeans, the backdrop often shadowy alleys or dimly lit streets.

"She's really leaning into this side of her personality," Clo murmured, scrolling through the posts. "Look at all this. The band merch, the black hoodies... She's telling the world exactly who she wants to be."

Grimshaw's eyes scanned the screen, as though searching for something beneath the surface of each image. The pictures showed Molly in heavy boots and dark clothes, a visual narrative of someone asserting her individuality—but maybe also hiding from something deeper. Band posters and selfies filled the feed. Some of the photos had captions that hinted at the frustration and isolation Molly felt, but nothing screamed for help.

Grimshaw's voice was thoughtful yet tinged with concern. "She's been posting a lot of herself lately. It's almost like she's trying to convince the world—or maybe herself—who she is."

Clo nodded, her eyes narrowing as she clicked through several pictures in quick succession. "Look at this. A user by the name of DarkSeraphim started showing up in the comments about two months ago—right around the same time as that diary entry."

Grimshaw leaned closer, his gaze sharpening. Sure enough, the username DarkSeraphim appeared beneath most of Molly's recent posts. The pattern was unsettling. Their comments appeared only on photos where Molly was the focal point. Band posters and scenic shots went uncommented. But every time Molly's face was visible, DarkSeraphim was there.

Clo frowned, her discomfort growing. "They're only interested in photos of her. Not the bands, not the things she's into. Just her."

The comments seemed innocuous at first, but as Clo scrolled through more of them, a more unsettling pattern emerged:

DarkSeraphim: Love the hoodie, GothGirl2010. You've got such a killer style.

DarkSeraphim: That jacket looks amazing on you.

Grimshaw's tone darkened. "Compliments. They're focusing on her appearance, making her feel noticed."

Clo's grip on the mouse tightened as unease settled in her chest. "They're laying it on thick. It's subtle at first, but they're making her feel seen, building her up—but only when she's in the frame. It's like her identity doesn't matter unless she's physically in the picture.

Clo navigated to Molly's direct messages, her fingers moving swiftly over the keyboard. It didn't take long to find DarkSeraphim's messages—they started around the same time as the Instagram comments. Clo clicked on the first exchange and began reading aloud:

DarkSeraphim: Hey, just saw your latest post. That black hoodie? It looks amazing on you.

GothGirl2010: Thanks! It's one of my favourites.

At first, the conversation was light, almost harmless. DarkSeraphim continued to compliment Molly's style, and Molly responded with shy appreciation. The messages were friendly, but there was an underlying familiarity, a warmth that felt out of place between strangers.

But as Clo scrolled further, the tone shifted. DarkSeraphim began to move beyond compliments, steering the conversation into more personal territory.

DarkSeraphim: You've got great taste in clothes and music. Me and my friends are into the same stuff. You'd totally fit in with us—we're like a family.

Clo's frown deepened. "They're starting to lay the groundwork. They're making her feel like she belongs with them. Like she's finally found her place."

Grimshaw's voice was low, tension creeping into his words. "They're building trust. Slowly isolating her from the people in her real life, making her feel like they're the only ones who understand her."

The messages continued, growing more intimate and more personal. DarkSeraphim began to play on Molly's insecurities, offering her a way out from the loneliness that surrounded her.

DarkSeraphim: It's tough, right? Feeling like no one at school really gets you. But I do. I understand you.

GothGirl2010: Yeah. It feels like I'm always out of place. Like no one sees me.

DarkSeraphim: But I see you. And my friends would love to meet you. We're all like you—part of the same circle. You'd fit in with us no problem.

Clo's stomach twisted as the gravity of the situation settled over her. "They're manipulating her. This isn't just friendship—it's like grooming. They're making her feel like she's finally found people who care about her."

Grimshaw's expression darkened further. "They're pulling her deeper into their world, offering her something no one else can. That kind of connection can be intoxicating, especially for someone who feels isolated."

The conversation shifted again, this time with DarkSeraphim offering Molly something more tangible—an escape.

DarkSeraphim: We're going to this amazing gig next month. You should come. I've got connections—I can get us backstage passes. Imagine meeting the band!

Clo's disgust was palpable. "They're luring her in with things she can't resist. Gigs, meeting bands, the whole scene. They're dangling a perfect life in front of her."

Grimshaw's voice was cold, measured. "They're offering her something no one else has—a place where she belongs. They're making her feel special."

As Clo scrolled deeper into the messages, it became clear that DarkSeraphim was no mere fan. They were using Molly's insecurities and her loneliness to push her toward something far more dangerous.

DarkSeraphim: I know you've thought about running away. If you ever do, you've got a place with us. You don't have to face it alone.

GothGirl2010: I don't know… it's scary.

DarkSeraphim: You don't need to be scared. We've got you. You'll be free with us.

Clo's heart sank as she read the final message. "They're setting her up to run. This isn't just grooming—it's a calculated move to take her in."

Before Grimshaw could respond, something clicked in Clo's mind. She reached for Molly's diary, flipping through the pages until she found the entry about someone she had been talking to online. She read aloud, her voice soft but tense.

There's someone I've been talking to online. They're different from anyone I've ever met. They understand me in ways no one else does.

Clo looked up at Grim, her expression grave. "This person is more than just a friend to her. They're offering her an escape. And she's already falling for it."

Grimshaw's voice was hard, filled with determination. "We need to trace this account. ASAP, we don't have much time."

Clo nodded, her fingers moving quickly over the keyboard. "I'll get Digital Forensics on it. We need to find out who this person really is."

The tension in the room mounted as the reality of the situation sank in. Molly was possibly in more danger than just a teenager who had run away from home

Grimshaw watched the screen as Clo worked, his mind racing. DarkSeraphim was no stranger. They were someone who had been carefully planning, carefully waiting. And now, they had Molly right where they wanted her.

Grimshaw muttered, his voice grim. "We have to find her before anything happens and it's too late."

Chapter 6: The Web

It was 8:30 a.m. on a crisp morning in Seaham. The sun hung low, casting a golden hue over the town's rugged coastline. Waves crashed against the cliffs, their rhythmic pounding echoing like a distant warning. The seaside town was calm, its early morning tranquillity offering a stark contrast to the dark currents swirling beneath the surface.

Inside a bright and airy internet café, life hummed with the usual bustle of morning activity. Customers lined up for their coffee, baristas exchanged pleasantries, and the faint murmur of conversation filled the air as patrons eased into their day. The café was busy enough to feel anonymous, exactly the way DarkSeraphim liked it.

They ordered a coffee, their manner polite, unremarkable—just another face in the crowd. The barista barely acknowledged them, eyes already moving on to the next customer in line.

Coffee in hand, DarkSeraphim moved to a corner table, tucked away from view but with a clear line of sight to the entrance. It was a routine they had perfected—always stay aware, always stay in control. They opened their laptop, sleek and unassuming, its dark screen reflecting the golden morning light. A few clicks later, the ping of a VPN activation masked their digital footprint, bouncing their signal around the globe. To anyone tracking them, they could be anywhere but here, in this quiet coastal town.

With the technicalities handled, they opened four tabs, each holding a conversation with different individuals. Four separate webs carefully spun, each person on the other end being reeled in, one by one. Each conversation had its own rhythm and its own tone. But the methods were always the same—compliments, trust, slow manipulation.

But today, only one tab held their true focus.

GothGirl2010.

Their fingers hovered above the keyboard as a flicker of excitement stirred within them. The others were distractions, secondary to their primary goal. GothGirl2010—Molly—was different. This wasn't just another game. This wasn't about collecting another trophy. DarkSeraphim felt something with Molly that they didn't with the others. A deeper need, a stronger pull. They needed her closer. And soon.

They scrolled through the conversation thread, tracing the evolution of their interactions over the past two months. It had all started innocently enough—comments on Molly's Instagram posts, specifically the ones where she showcased her style: dark hoodies, ripped jeans, heavy boots. They had watched her carefully before reaching out, waiting for the perfect moment to strike.

Molly's posts were filled with heavy symbolism, moody images, and band logos. It was clear she was leaning heavily into her gothic identity, trying to express something—perhaps trying to prove something to herself.

Thinking back, DarkSeraphim remembered how their fingers had danced across the keyboard, the familiar rush of control filling them as they typed. It always started like this—innocent, subtle, pulling them in one whisper at a time. Molly had been no different. She was just another mark, another lost soul. The thrill of the hunt never got old, especially with the ones who fought back, the ones who resisted. It was almost too easy to twist them, to break them.

They think they can see through me. But they never do.

A small smile tugged at the corner of DarkSeraphim's lips as they recalled Molly's early responses—unsure, vulnerable. She was the perfect type. So many others had come before her, and just like them, Molly would fall too. But it was important to keep things controlled. Always controlled.

Except that one time…

DarkSeraphim's fingers paused for a moment, a memory flickering to life. Cornwall. It had been too close. A girl had slipped through their fingers—too late to save, but almost enough to ruin everything. The investigation had nearly uncovered them. A Detective by the name of Grimshaw had been too close.

But not this time. Grimshaw wasn't here at the other end of the country.

DarkSeraphim shook off the thought, refocusing on the task at hand. They clicked into the direct messages with Molly, where the real connection had started to take shape.

DarkSeraphim: You look incredible in that new pic, GothGirl2010. Love the jeans. Seriously, you look amazing, you've got the best style.

It had been so easy to hook her with compliments. A few well-placed words, enough to make her feel noticed. Molly had responded eagerly, flattered by the attention.

Now, they scrolled through the messages, each one bringing Molly deeper into their web.

DarkSeraphim: You've got great taste in clothes and music. Me and my friends are into the same stuff. You'd totally fit in with us—we're like a family.

That was the key. Family. DarkSeraphim had quickly realized that this was what Molly craved most—a sense of belonging, of being understood. They had played into that need perfectly, offering her what she wasn't getting from her friends or family.

They typed a new message, their fingers moving swiftly and confidently across the keys.

DarkSeraphim: That last pic you posted? Killer outfit. You really know how to pull it all together. Wish you were here with us—we'd be at gigs all the time. You'd fit right in.

They hit send, leaning back in their chair as they took a slow sip of coffee. This was just another step forward, another link in the chain that was slowly pulling Molly closer. DarkSeraphim knew Molly was already teetering on the edge, but patience was key. Rushing things now would spoil everything.

A notification blinked on another tab—a message from one of the others. They clicked on it briefly, typing a short reply to maintain the illusion of attention. But their focus never wavered from GothGirl2010. The others were routine, part of the process. But Molly? Molly was the prize.

They returned to Molly's conversation, scrolling back to the moment when the messages had shifted from casual flattery to something deeper.

DarkSeraphim: It must be tough, feeling like you don't fit in anywhere. But I get it. I feel the same way sometimes. That's why I like talking to you—you understand me too.

That had been the turning point. Molly had opened up more than they had anticipated. She had shared her frustrations and her isolation, and DarkSeraphim had been there to catch her, offering comfort and understanding—everything she wasn't getting from the people around her.

Their fingers moved quickly, typing another message designed to feed into the emotional bond they had carefully nurtured.

DarkSeraphim: You deserve to be with people who get you. Me and my friends? We're the same. We're like a family. You'd love it with us—we all listen to the same music and go to the same gigs. I've got connections. We get backstage passes all the time. Imagine meeting the band.

They leaned back again, satisfied. This message would ignite Molly's curiosity and her desire to belong. DarkSeraphim knew exactly how to play this game—offering her the one thing she craved most: acceptance. And now, with this invitation, they had begun to reel her in even further.

They glanced at another tab, firing off a quick response to one of the other conversations. But it was mechanical, their mind fully focused on Molly. She was different. She was special.

And then there was the matter of the missed opportunity.

It was supposed to happen the previous Saturday. GothGirl2010 had agreed to meet them. Everything had been arranged, the plan set in motion. But at the last minute, Molly had cancelled. Her father had forced her to go to a sleepover at Sarah's house, against Molly's wishes. Molly hadn't wanted to be there, surrounded by girls who represented everything she despised.

DarkSeraphim's fingers tapped lightly on the table, frustration bubbling beneath the surface. They rarely allowed themselves to feel emotions like this, but the cancellation had thrown a wrench into their carefully laid plans. Molly had been so close—so close—and now they had to wait.

They typed a quick reply to one of the other tabs, keeping up appearances. But their mind remained on Molly. The disappointment, the irritation of having to pause what was so close to becoming reality.

Then, a notification pinged.

A message from GothGirl2010.

The surge of excitement was immediate, but DarkSeraphim tempered it. They wouldn't open the message right away. Letting Molly stew a little and feel the weight of the missed opportunity, would work in their favour. She needed to feel the uncertainty, the fear of losing their connection.

Another notification.

Then another.

Three messages from Molly, waiting to be opened. But DarkSeraphim resisted the urge to click. Instead, they continued replying to the other conversations, each response feeling more mechanical than the last. Their attention was divided, but only by the growing anticipation of Molly's messages.

After fifteen calculated minutes, they finally clicked on Molly's first message.

GothGirl2010: I'm really sorry about Saturday. My dad made me go to this stupid sleepover at Sarah's house. I didn't even want to be there. Please don't be upset with me.

The second message appeared immediately after.

GothGirl2010: I didn't mean to let you down. I really want to meet you and your friends. Please don't ignore me.

And the third, the most desperate of all.

GothGirl2010: Please don't forget about me. I feel so bad. I won't let it happen again.

DarkSeraphim smiled.

Molly was apologizing, begging for forgiveness. She was right where they wanted her—desperate to keep the connection alive. Desperate not to lose what she thought was her only lifeline. DarkSeraphim had the upper hand now. They could use this to make her feel like she had to prove herself like she needed to do more to earn their attention.

They typed a response, measured and controlled.

DarkSeraphim: I get it. Things happen. Just don't leave me hanging again, okay? We're still here for you whenever you're ready but we won't wait forever.

They hit send, feeling the power shift back into place. Molly was slipping further away from her old life, and soon she would be theirs completely.

In the bright sunlight of the café, DarkSeraphim sat back, satisfied. Molly was already entangled in their web, and soon there would be no escape.

Chapter 7: The Clock is Ticking

Washington Station was already bustling when Grimshaw and Clo walked through the doors at 7:30 a.m. Despite leaving just after 2:30 a.m. the night before. The station was alive with the familiar hum of ringing phones and low voices. Officers shuffled past in various states of exhaustion, but Grim and Clo were laser-focused, driven by the ticking clock on Molly's case. Exhausted, yes, but the weight of urgency kept them moving.

They didn't bother with small talk, opting instead to grab a couple of coffees on their way to their desks. Both detectives wore the same clothes as the day before, the long hours etched in their faces. But the case was all that mattered. They couldn't afford to slow down now.

As they approached their desks, Chief Superintendent Adams's office door swung open. His sharp eyes locked onto them from across the room. "Grimshaw! Harper! In here, now."

Clo glanced at Grim, who gave a quick nod. They had been expecting this—an update on their progress was overdue. They grabbed their notes and hurried toward Adams's office, the urgency in his voice leaving no room for delay.

Once inside, Adams didn't waste time. His desk was cluttered with paperwork and case files, but his focus was entirely on them. "I want everything. We've got a missing girl and I want an update."

Grimshaw's expression remained neutral, his tone steady but serious as he spoke. "We went to Molly Reid's home yesterday morning. There's a clear disconnect between Molly and her father, Paul Reid. He's been pushing her to conform—wants her to be more 'normal,' more like the other girls her age. But Molly… she's different. She's been struggling to express her identity, and that tension's been building for a while."

Clo picked up where Grim left off. "Molly's isolated. She's pulled away from her friends, even from her family. When we spoke to her friend Sarah, who's sleepover she attended the night before she disappeared, It was clear she didn't fit in with Sarah or the other girls. She spent most of the night alone on her phone and left early the next morning without saying much."

Adams's brow furrowed as he absorbed the details. "Any signs of foul play from the friend? Anything unusual at the sleepover?"

Clo shook her head. "Nothing suspicious at the sleepover, just that Molly was out of place. But what stands out is what we found in Molly's room. Her phone—left behind. It was packed with missed calls from her mother, but there was no communication from her father. The biggest lead came from her diary which we also found in her room which has led us to her social media."

"Hold on I thought you said she spent the night on her phone" stated Adams, "yes" replied Grim, "it appears that she had a second phone, Sarah confirmed that it was a different brand to her usual phone" he continued.

Grimshaw leaned forward, his tone sharpening. "after checking her phone we found messages from someone using the handle 'DarkSeraphim' on her Instagram account. They've been in contact for two months. It started with casual compliments about Molly's appearance, particularly when she posted pictures of herself."

Clo added, "It started innocently praising her clothes, her style, making her feel seen. But it escalated into something more sinister. DarkSeraphim built up trust, made Molly feel like they understood her, and then began offering her something she desperately needed—a place where she could belong. They used Molly's love of music to lure her in, promising gigs and backstage passes."

Adams's face hardened as the details sank in. "They're grooming her."

"Exactly," Clo confirmed. "They're isolating her emotionally, making her feel like her only option is to leave home and meet them. We found a trail that led to DarkSeraphim arranging a new phone for Molly to use to contact them outside of her parent's eyes"

Grimshaw's voice remained calm, but his intensity was unmistakable. "Molly was clearly reluctant about the sleepover. She had no connection to Sarah's friends and no interest in being there. We believe the phone that she was using was the one that DarkSeraphim had arranged for her and it was a way for her to keep in touch"

Adams stood up, pacing behind his desk. His frustration was palpable. "This person has been manipulating Molly, cutting her off from her family and friends. So, what are we doing to find Molly and this DarkSeraphim?"

"We've got Digital Forensics working on tracking DarkSeraphim's messages," Clo said. "They're using a VPN to mask their location, but we've requested a trace. It'll take time to break through."

Adams crossed his arms, his eyes narrowing. "Time's not on our side. Molly's been missing for almost two days now. DarkSeraphim's potentially dangerous. We need to stop this before it's too late."

Grimshaw nodded, his voice resolute. "We will, sir."

"Good." Adams's tone was final. "And don't waste a minute."

Dismissed, Grim and Clo left the office with the weight of the investigation bearing down on them. There was no room for error now—Molly's life was in their hands, and they knew it.

Back at their desks, Clo immediately logged on to the computer with the digital forensic link to Molly's phone while Grimshaw silently reviewed their notes. Every detail mattered now. They had gone over Molly's messages, her Instagram profile, and her diary entries multiple times, but they couldn't afford to miss anything. Grim's sharp eyes picked up on the subtleties—the slow, methodical way DarkSeraphim had drawn Molly into their web. It all felt too familiar for him, but he kept it to himself.

Clo scrolled through Molly's Instagram messages again, frustration evident in her voice. "Nothing. We've gone through every post and every message, and still nothing solid about who or where DarkSeraphim is. It's like trying to find a tree that a leaf has fallen off, we know the type of tree but not the exact location"

Grim's jaw tightened, his frustration barely contained. "They've been planning this for months, Clo. If Molly's already made up her mind, we might only have hours before she disappears for good, that is if she hasn't already."

Clo was about to respond when her phone buzzed loudly on the desk. She glanced at the screen, her pulse quickening. "It's an alert from Digital Forensics."

Grimshaw moved to her side, his eyes locked on the monitor. "What are we looking at?"

Clo clicked into the alert, her eyes widening as she saw the notification. "We've got new messages. Molly's Instagram. These are happening now."

Grimshaw leaned in closer, his voice low and tense. "She's messaging in real-time?"

Clo nodded, her voice tight with urgency. "This isn't old data. These messages are coming through right now."

The first message appeared on the screen:

GothGirl2010: I'm so sorry about the weekend. My dad made me go to the sleepover. I didn't want to be there. Please don't be mad.

Clo exchanged a glance with Grimshaw, her heart pounding. "Is she apologising for not meeting up? It's like she's trying to smooth things over with DarkSeraphim."

Another message from Molly appeared almost immediately:

GothGirl2010: You have to believe me. I didn't want to go. I don't care about Sarah or her friends. You're the only one who understands me. Please don't ignore me.

Grimshaw's voice was steady, but there was an edge to it. "She's scared. She thinks DarkSeraphim might cut her off."

Clo frowned; her eyes glued to the screen. "She's desperate to keep them on her side."

The seconds ticked by, but there was no response from DarkSeraphim. The silence was deafening. Clo glanced at the clock, anxiety gnawing at her. "Why aren't they responding? It's been too long."

Grimshaw's voice was quiet, his tone dark with understanding. "They're making her sweat. It's a power play. They want her to feel uncertain like she's on thin ice. It'll make her even more dependent on them when they finally reply."

Clo nodded, recognizing the manipulation at play. "They're keeping her on edge. It's classic control."

More minutes passed, the silence between Molly and DarkSeraphim growing heavier. Then, another message from Molly appeared on the screen, her desperation clear:

GothGirl2010: Please say something. Don't leave me hanging like this. I need you.

Clo's face tightened; her voice filled with concern. "This is getting worse. She's spiralling."

Grimshaw's eyes narrowed as the realization struck him. He straightened suddenly, turning to Clo with a sense of urgency. "How's she sending these messages?" → she had another phone. what are you?

Clo blinked, confused. "What do you mean?" Kind of detective

Grimshaw's expression was firm, his voice low. "Molly's phone. We have it. It's in evidence, Christ we're looking at it right now!"

Clo's eyes widened as she realized what he was getting at. "You're right. So how is she sending these messages? Her parents didn't say anything about a laptop or a tablet"

Grim stood up, pacing as his mind raced. "This must be the device Sarah mentioned. The phone Molly was using at the sleepover."

aha you remembered ←

Clo immediately grabbed her own phone, dialling Digital Forensics. Her voice was tense as she spoke into the receiver. "This is Harper. Can we trace the location of the device sending these new messages on Molly's Instagram account?"

She listened intently, her expression growing more focused by the second. "Right, do it as fast as you can. This needs to be a priority."

Hanging up, Clo turned to Grimshaw, her expression tight with urgency. "They're on it. If we can trace this device, we might finally get a location."

Grimshaw nodded, his face unreadable but determined. "This is our best chance. We're getting close."

As they waited for the trace, both of them knew the clock was ticking faster than ever. Molly was slipping further into DarkSeraphim's grip, and they had to act before it was too late.

Chapter 8: Too Close for Comfort

The tinkling of the bell above the café door was a small comfort to Molly as she stepped inside. Her hair was a tangled mess, and her clothes, wrinkled and stained, betrayed the fact that she had spent two nights sleeping rough. Her movements were slow, every step weighed down by exhaustion, and her eyes darted nervously around the room, as though she both expected and hoped to remain unnoticed.

The café was a welcome contrast to the chaos Molly felt inside. The air was warm and filled with the comforting scent of coffee and pastries. Conversations hummed softly around her, creating a background of normality that seemed alien to her current state of mind.

The barista behind the counter glanced up, recognition flickering in his eyes. Molly had been in the day before, looking just as tired and dishevelled as she did now. Despite her appearance, the barista offered her a kind smile, one that was filled with quiet concern.

"Hey, you're back," he said softly, leaning slightly over the counter, his tone gentle and non-intrusive. "Everything alright?"

Molly hesitated, unsure of how to respond. The last thing she wanted was to talk. She didn't have the energy for small talk, let alone for explaining the growing storm inside her. "Just... tired," she muttered, her gaze fixed on the floor.

The barista nodded sympathetically. "I get that," he said, his voice soothing. "You need anything? Coffee, sandwich? We just got a fresh batch out."

Molly's hand dipped into her pocket, her fingers closing around the few coins she had left. It wasn't much—barely enough for a coffee, or maybe a small bite to eat but not both. She weighed her options, feeling the familiar gnaw of hunger clawing at her stomach. "Coffee," she whispered, then, almost as an afterthought, "actually no a sandwich."

The barista moved swiftly, preparing her order. When he handed her the coffee and a sandwich wrapped in white paper, he added with a small smile, "On the house today."

Surprise flickered across Molly's face. She wasn't used to kindness, not like this. For a brief moment, she almost smiled back, but the emotion flickered and vanished before it could fully form. "Thanks," she mumbled, taking her food and retreating toward a booth at the back of the café. With her back to a person who was muttering to themselves and typing away on a keyboard

In the booth behind Molly, DarkSeraphim sat hunched over their laptop. Multiple tabs blinked on the screen, each holding a conversation with different targets. They were entirely engrossed in their work—manipulating and guiding each person like a puppet master pulling strings. Each conversation followed a familiar pattern, carefully calibrated for maximum effect. Every move had a purpose.

Molly, completely unaware of the proximity of the person who had been her comfort, her support her only port in what felt like a tropical storm, sat in the booth directly behind them. Her exhaustion blinded her to everything except the buzz of her phone as she plugged it into the charger. Her hands trembled as the phone began to charge

There it was—the message she had been waiting for.

DarkSeraphim: You don't have to keep pretending. We're here for you whenever you're ready.

Molly stared at the message, her heart pounding. Her fingers shook as she read the words, her relief almost overwhelming. She had felt so lost, so invisible. But DarkSeraphim saw her—they understood her in ways no one else ever had. Not her dad. Not Sarah. No one.

She quickly typed out her response, the words spilling out of her in a rush:

GothGirl2010: I didn't want to go to that sleepover. My dad made me. I don't care about Sarah or her friends. They don't understand me like you do.

She hit send and stared at the screen, her pulse racing. DarkSeraphim had become her anchor, her only real connection in a world that felt more alien every day. They were the only ones who didn't judge her, who didn't make her feel like she had to change. They accepted her for who she was.

In the booth behind her, DarkSeraphim smiled as they saw Molly had read the message.

Molly's response had been expected, and DarkSeraphim felt a thrill of satisfaction. She was teetering on the edge now, just close enough to fall completely under their influence. But it wasn't time to push just yet. The timing was everything. Too much pressure now, and she might hesitate. Too little, and they might lose her entirely.

They typed again, more slowly this time:

DarkSeraphim: We understand you, Molly. You don't have to pretend with us. We're like a family. Didn't we prove that when we gave you the new phone, so we can talk just us and no one else?

Molly's heart raced as she read the message. The promise of belonging, of finally being understood, was so tempting, almost too good to be true. But she hesitated, her fingers hovering over the keys.

GothGirl2010: That sounds amazing. I just... I don't know. I'm scared.

DarkSeraphim's smile widened. Perfect.

They typed back, taking their time, knowing they had her now.

DarkSeraphim: You don't need to be scared. We'll take care of everything. Just say the word, and we'll get you out of there. You'll be safe with us, Molly. Trust me.

Molly stared at the screen, her heart thudding painfully in her chest. It was the escape she had been longing for—an invitation to leave behind everything that made her feel trapped, lonely, and misunderstood. But still, something held her back. She was so close to taking the leap, but fear and doubt gnawed at her.

Across the booth, DarkSeraphim watched the screen, their fingers twitching in anticipation. It was only a matter of time before Molly would be theirs. Soon, she would take that final step, and there would be no turning back.

Back at Washington Station

Grimshaw and Clo sat in the dimly lit office, the glow of the computer screens casting a pale light over their faces. They had been watching Molly's online interactions for what felt like hours, piecing together the horrifying reality of DarkSeraphim's manipulation. Every message, every conversation was another thread in the web that had ensnared Molly.

Grimshaw's jaw clenched as he read the messages. "She's completely reliant on them. DarkSeraphim has isolated her from everyone else."

Clo scrolled further, her expression tightening. "Look at this. DarkSeraphim is reminding Molly about the phone: 'Didn't we prove that when we gave you the new phone so we can talk just us and no one else?'"

Grimshaw froze. his eyes narrowing. "So it was them that gave her the new phone?"

Grimshaw ran a hand through his hair, frustration clear in his voice. "How did DarkSeraphim get Molly a new phone? If she's messaging them right now, it has to be through that device."

Then, just as Grimshaw was about to speak, Clo's phone rang, its sharp tone cutting through the heavy silence. She answered quickly.

"Harper."

The voice on the other end was clear. "We've traced the second device. It's active right now, coming from a café in Seaham."

Clo's pulse quickened. "Seaham? That's only about thirty minutes away."

Grimshaw didn't hesitate. "Let's go. Now."

Clo grabbed her jacket, her heart pounding as she spoke quickly into the phone. "We're on our way. Keep monitoring the signal." As they left the office Clo shouted at one of the juniors to contact Durham Constabulary, "Seaham is their patch let them know what is happening"

As they rushed out of the station, Grimshaw's mind raced. If DarkSeraphim was with Molly at that café, this could be their only chance to stop them. But time was running out. They needed to act fast—before it was too late.

Chapter 9: Too Close to See

The bell above the café door jingled as Molly stepped outside, her hair dishevelled, her clothes rumpled from two nights of sleeping rough. Every muscle in her body ached from the hours spent curled up in dark, uncomfortable corners. She kept her head down, hoping her worn appearance would blend in with the city's busy backdrop.

Outside, the streets bustled with early morning commuters and shoppers moving through their day with purpose, while Molly drifted aimlessly, her mind swirling with a cocktail of fear and confusion. The sounds of clattering footsteps, snippets of conversation, and honking cars echoed around her, but Molly felt miles away from it all. A part of her longed to just disappear into the sea of faces, but another part—the part DarkSeraphim had cultivated—kept her alert. She couldn't afford to relax. Someone might be looking for her, following her. The paranoia clung to her like a straight jacket.

Her phone buzzed in her pocket, snapping her out of her thoughts. Another message from DarkSeraphim.

DarkSeraphim: Did you leave your other phone at home, or do you still have it with you?

Molly frowned at the question, her stomach twisting with a mixture of anxiety and confusion. What did it matter where her old phone was? DarkSeraphim had already told her the new phone was enough. The old one was obsolete now. Still, she responded:

GothGirl2010: I left it at home. Why?

The reply came almost immediately:

DarkSeraphim: I think your dad's tracking you. He's getting close. You need to be careful, Molly. I can help, but you have to stay away from places where people might recognize you.

The blood drained from Molly's face as the words sank in. Is her father tracking her? The idea felt suffocating, like a net tightening around her. She had run away to escape his control, to get away from the constant pressure to be someone she wasn't. The thought that he could be using technology to find her made her chest tighten with panic.

Her dad had always been overbearing and strict, but would he really go this far? Molly didn't doubt it. She had always been a problem in his eyes, a disappointment. He was probably furious right now, ready to drag her back and lock her up in his perfectly polished world where she didn't belong. The phone in her hand felt like her only connection to safety.

GothGirl2010: Where should I go? she typed, her hands shaking.

As Molly crossed the street towards Tommy (the big war memorial in the centre of Seaham) Grimshaw and Clo stepped through the café door, their eyes scanning the room, tension radiating off them. The peaceful hum of the café felt jarring compared to the urgency pounding in their chests. They moved through the space with purpose, knowing every second counted.

Clo was the first to approach the barista, her voice low but urgent as she flashed her badge. "Sergeant Harper, Washington Station," she said, her words cutting through the soft murmur of the café. "We're looking for a teenage girl. Dark hair, mid-teens. Was she in here recently?"

The barista blinked, caught off guard by the abruptness of the question. "Uh, yeah," he said after a moment, pointing toward an empty booth in the back. "She was sitting right over there. Looked pretty out of it."

Grimshaw's eyes flicked toward the booth, a heavy knot forming in his stomach as he took in the sight of the empty seat. "How long ago?" he asked, his tone clipped.

"Maybe ten minutes? She didn't stay long."

Grimshaw clenched his jaw, frustration surging through him. They had been so close. Molly had been right here, practically within arm's reach. And now, she was gone. "She's on the move," he muttered to Clo. "We need to find her."

Clo nodded, glancing down at her phone. "Let me check in with Forensics and see if they've got an update on her location." She stepped outside the café, dialling the number with shaky fingers.

Grimshaw remained inside, scanning the café for any other clues, any signs of Molly's presence. His gaze was hard, his thoughts racing. The longer Molly stayed out there, the more dangerous things would get. DarkSeraphim had her in their grip, and it was only a matter of time before they pulled her deeper into their web.

Across the café, seated quietly in a corner booth, DarkSeraphim looked over to the counter at the sound of Sargent Clo introducing herself had remained unnoticed. They watched the officers with calculated calm, their heart pounding but their expressions betraying nothing.

Their laptop was packed away now, the carefully crafted persona hidden from the world. DarkSeraphim's mind raced with possibilities and contingency plans. The police were closing in, but they hadn't connected the dots. Not yet. Molly was still within their reach. DarkSeraphim stood and crossed the café towards the door, Grimshaw opened the door and their eyes met for a fleeting second and they both felt a small amount of recognition like a face in a crowd catching your eye but the moment passed almost as quickly as it had come.

In the middle of the crowded square, Molly's phone buzzed again, pulling her attention back to the small device in her hand. Another message from DarkSeraphim appeared on the screen this time through a text message:

DarkSeraphim: Download this VPN app. It'll keep you hidden. Your dad won't be able to track you anymore.

[handwritten annotation with arrow pointing to above message: This makes no sense as her Dad is supposedly using her old phone, so VPN would need to be on that one.]

Molly hesitated for a moment, her finger hovering over the message. The idea of her dad tracking her through her phone sent a chill down her spine, and the thought of hiding from him, of staying out of his reach, was too tempting to resist. She quickly downloaded the app, her anxiety mounting with every passing second. She replied to the message confirming she had done it.

DarkSeraphim: Good. You're safe now. Just keep moving. Find somewhere quiet, somewhere no one will recognize you.

Molly glanced around, her gaze flitting nervously from one face to the next. Her heart raced as paranoia set in. Was someone watching her? Had her dad really gone this far? Every man in a suit and every woman in heels looked like a potential threat. She pulled her hood up tighter, turning away from Tommy and crossed the busy streets, seeking the quieter, less crowded paths. She needed to disappear.

Her phone buzzed again, another message from DarkSeraphim.

DarkSeraphim: tell me where you are and I will guide you to safety.

I am in Seaham, my dad doesn't like the place so I felt it was the safest place, and I like being by the sea. Responded Molly

Seaham? Hang on that explained the police. If Molly was really that close, how could they not have known that, thought DarkSeraphim

Head to the harbour. It's quiet there, and no one will find you. I'll meet you soon.

Molly's stomach churned at the thought of heading to the harbour. It was isolated, and cold, a part of town where no one would look for her. It also sounded dangerous. But what choice did she have? DarkSeraphim had been right about everything else. They had guided her through this mess and helped her escape her father's reach. She couldn't stop trusting them now.

Her feet moved faster, carrying her toward the waterfront with growing urgency. She had to stay ahead of her dad. If she stopped now, it would all come crashing down. The dockyards loomed in the distance and the smell of saltwater already faintly in the air of the seaside town was getting stronger.

Meanwhile, Clo's phone rang, pulling her attention back to the situation at hand. Digital Forensics was on the line, their voices tense as they relayed the latest update.

"We've lost Molly's signal," the technician said, his voice tight with frustration. "looks like she has activated a VPN. We can't track her anymore. Also, the Instagram messages have stopped. They have either met up or switched to another messaging service. I will send over the last messages"

Clo's heart sank. "A VPN?" she repeated, her mind racing. "DarkSeraphim must have told her to use it." Clo felt the phone buzz in her hand as she ended the call, she turned to Grim and said this is the last message,

DarkSeraphim: Did you leave your other phone at home, or do you still have it with you?

GothGirl2010: I left it at home. Why?

DarkSeraphim: I think your dad's tracking you. He's getting close. You need to be careful, Molly. I can help, but you have to stay away from places where people might recognize you.

GothGirl2010: Where should I go? she typed, her hands shaking.

Grimshaw, reading the messages, clenched his fists. "They're covering their tracks. DarkSeraphim knows we're onto them. But how?"

Clo ran a hand through her hair, her frustration mounting. "What do we do now, Grim? Without the trace, we're flying blind. Molly could be anywhere."

Grimshaw's expression hardened, determination setting in. "We think like her. She's scared. She thinks her dad's tracking her, and DarkSeraphim is telling her to disappear. They'll be guiding her to somewhere isolated, somewhere she can hide."

Clo's brow furrowed in thought. "The harbour or the train station," she said suddenly. "It's quiet out there, not many people, easy to hide. The only issue is we can't cover both as they are at opposite ends of the town, there is a police station just up the road from the train station. We could ask Durham Constabulary if they could send some over to look?"

Grimshaw nodded. "Good idea, you make the call, and we will head to the harbour, Let's move. We can't waste another minute."

Molly's footsteps echoed in the empty streets as she made her way toward the harbour, the sound of her shoes on the pavement a steady reminder of how far she'd come—and how alone she was. The sun was starting to rise higher in the sky, but the day felt grey, muted, as though the world had dimmed just for her.

The harbour loomed ahead, there was a smaller container ship and cranes casting long shadows over the water and just beyond that was the lighthouse. Molly pulled her hood up tighter, trying to shake off the gnawing unease in her stomach. She had trusted DarkSeraphim this far, but now that she was here, doubts crept in. The silence was unnerving, the isolation pressing down on her like a weight.

Her phone buzzed again, DarkSeraphim's message appearing on the screen:

DarkSeraphim: are you almost there? I'm close by.

Molly glanced around, but there was no sign of anyone else in the street she was moving down. The harbour was busy and she hoped when she got over to them she could blend into the crowd. A shiver ran down her spine, but she pushed forward, her legs heavy with exhaustion.

"Come on, Molly," she muttered to herself. "Just keep going."

But every step felt harder, every breath more laboured. Her mind raced with conflicting emotions—fear, doubt, hope. DarkSeraphim had promised her freedom, a way out. But was this it? Was this really the life she had wanted? At that moment she wasn't sure if the light that she could see at the end of the tunnel was the freedom she craved or the headlights of an oncoming train, either way, she needed to move, she needed to trust it was freedom.

Her father's voice echoed in her mind, his disappointment, his frustration with her never being the daughter he wanted. Her mind started to turn like the wheels on a train very slowly at first but gradually picking up speed, how was her father tracking her? How was that possible when she had left her phone, but also how did DarkSeraphim know? Had they seen him in the area? she stopped, her breath catching in her throat. She was too deep in it now to know what was real. She couldn't trust her father. She couldn't go back. But something about this situation felt wrong. A feeling of unease started to creep down her spine but she couldn't concentrate on that now and pushed it to the back of her mind.

Her phone buzzed again, another message lighting up the screen. But this time, Molly hesitated before opening it.

Chapter 10: Just Out of Reach

Molly stared at the screen, and read the message

DarkSeraphim: where are you? Are you close? Tell me remember I am here to help you be free

Molly hesitated before replying: I am just coming through the shopping centre, How do you know my dad's tracking me? How can you be sure?

A pause followed—long enough to make Molly feel a tightening in her chest. She half-expected the answer to be something that would scare her even more.

DarkSeraphim: Trust me, Molly. I've seen this before. Parents like him—controlling, overbearing—they'll do anything to keep you under their thumb. He's probably using every tool he can find to trace your steps.

Molly's fingers hovered over the keyboard as she processed the response. She wanted to believe DarkSeraphim, but something wasn't adding up. Her dad had always been strict, yes, but would he really go to such lengths to track her down? He wasn't exactly a tech expert. The doubt lingered in her mind, growing louder the more she thought about it. Was DarkSeraphim telling her the truth?

She swallowed hard, her anxiety mounting as she typed again:

GothGirl2010: But how do you know? I'm just scared. It doesn't make sense.

The response came swiftly, as though DarkSeraphim had anticipated her hesitation:

DarkSeraphim: I've dealt with people like him before. They always use technology to control their kids, to keep tabs on them. That's why I told you to download the VPN. You're safe with me, Molly. You have to trust me.

Molly's heart raced as she read the message. She didn't want to believe her dad would go this far, but she was also terrified of being caught. The more DarkSeraphim spoke, the more convincing they became. They had been right about so many things already. Could she really question them now?

Before she could reply, another message appeared:

DarkSeraphim: I am just parking in the harbour carpark, tell me when you are here

Sitting in the car, DarkSeraphim was thinking back to the café, After hearing the police talking in the café, their nerves were on high alert. They couldn't risk sticking around any longer, not with the authorities closing in. But as then, a new thought gnawed at them. If the person the barista had described was Molly then they hadn't noticed enter or leave the café earlier. She had been so close, and yet they hadn't even realized it.

They cursed under their breath, frustration rising. How had they missed her? Molly had been right under their nose, and they hadn't taken the opportunity to meet her. But no matter. They still had control. Molly was following their instructions, using the VPN and trusting them with everything. She was still in Seaham, and DarkSeraphim needed to make sure she didn't slip out of their grasp again.

They pulled out their phone, typing another message to Molly, their fingers moving quickly across the screen:

DarkSeraphim: You're doing great. Keep heading toward the harbour. We'll meet soon, and then you'll be safe.

Their eyes scanned the streets as they sent the message, paranoia bubbling beneath the surface. Were the police still watching? Could they be closing in on them now? DarkSeraphim wasn't sure, but they couldn't take any chances. They needed to meet Molly in person—it was the only way to pull her completely away from everything and disappear together. Risky, yes, but necessary.

Grimshaw and Clo moved quickly through Seaham's winding streets, their frustration mounting with each turn. Grim stared out the window, his mind working quickly through possible scenarios. "She's panicked," he said quietly, thinking out loud. "If she's still relying on DarkSeraphim for guidance, they'll tell her to lay low, to hide somewhere until they can meet. They'll push her further underground."

Grim's gaze darkened, his voice hardening with determination. "DarkSeraphim won't let her go far, not until they're ready to make their move. Molly's scared, vulnerable—she won't make any decisions without their input."

They moved through the shopping centre over the road from the harbour

At that moment Clo's phone rang, it was one of the officers from the Seaham station, "we are at the train station and there is no sign of the missing girl. We are speaking to security to see if we can check the CCTV"

Molly's feet ached from the constant movement, her mind swirling with exhaustion and fear. Another message from DarkSeraphim buzzed in her hand:

DarkSeraphim: You're doing great. Keep heading toward the harbour. We'll meet soon, and then you'll be safe.

Molly's chest tightened. She was so close to freedom, so close to escaping the world that had suffocated her for so long. But each step toward the harbour felt heavier, weighed down by doubt and fear. She couldn't shake the feeling that something was wrong.

Her phone buzzed again, but this time, she hesitated before looking at the message. Was this really what she wanted? Was DarkSeraphim really who they said they were?

Molly was at a crossroads—too close to the edge to turn back, but unsure if she could take the final leap.

Chapter 11: Unveiling the Shadows

Grimshaw and Clo left the shopping centre and moved to the road to cross over to the harbour, there were a few cars in the carpark and they could hear the hustle and bustle of the busy little harbour.

The sharp ring of Clo's phone shattered the stillness. She glanced at the caller ID and answered quickly—it was the station.

"Harper," she said, keeping her voice calm despite the mounting tension.

It was one of the officers from the station, their voice edged with concern. "Mrs. Reid's on the phone. She's been trying to reach you. Says her husband's been acting strange ever since your visit."

Clo's brow furrowed, exchanging a look with Grimshaw. "Strange how?" she asked, her tone sharp with curiosity.

The detective on the other end hesitated before continuing. "She said Paul's been disappearing since Molly went missing. Gone four hours, unreachable, and when she tries calling, his phone's off. She's worried something's going on."

Grimshaw's attention snapped to the conversation. He leaned in slightly, listening intently as Clo pressed further. "Did she say where he's been going?"

"No," the detective replied. "But she's adamant it's not like him."

Clo shared a glance with Grimshaw. Paul Reid had been distant during their initial visit, but disappearing for hours with his phone turned off? That raised more questions than it answered.

"Alright," Clo said, her mind spinning through the implications. "Tell Mrs Reid we'll follow up. We're still focused on finding Molly, but we'll look into it."

As she ended the call, Grimshaw ran a hand through his hair. "Paul Reid's been acting strange. That's not a coincidence."

Before they could delve deeper into the possibilities, Clo's phone buzzed again. This time, it was Samantha Crews—Sam, one of the junior detectives assigned to go through Molly's diary entries.

"Sam, what have you got?" Clo asked, sensing the urgency in Sam's tone.

Sam's voice was steady but laced with concern. "We found some entries in Molly's diary from about six months ago—and even earlier. They suggest something... disturbing."

Grimshaw leaned closer, his eyes narrowing. Clo put the call on speaker so they could both hear.

"Disturbing how?" Clo asked, her stomach tightening in anticipation.

Sam took a deep breath before continuing. "Molly wrote about one of her dad's female friends. She doesn't name her, but it's clear this woman was making Molly uncomfortable. The conversations Molly described were suggestive—not explicitly sexual, but close. The woman was commenting on how Molly was 'growing up fast,' making remarks about her appearance. Molly didn't seem to fully understand it, but she knew something was off."

Grimshaw's expression darkened. Clo's mind started to spin, the weight of Sam's words sinking in. "Molly was being manipulated," Clo muttered more to herself than to Sam.

Sam's voice grew more serious. "It looks that way. The entries show a gradual escalation in this woman's behaviour. Molly didn't want to be around her, but her dad encouraged their interactions. But here's the thing—the entries stop abruptly about two months ago."

Grimshaw and Clo exchanged a glance. "That's around the same time Molly started changing talking to DarkSeraphim," Grimshaw said, piecing together the timeline.

Sam's voice softened. "Yeah. Maybe the attention stopped or maybe she was blocking it out."

Clo's voice grew sharper. "And Paul Reid? He never intervened?"

"No," Sam said, the frustration clear in her voice. "According to the diary, he didn't seem to notice—or didn't want to."

"Thanks, Sam," Clo said. "Keep digging through those entries and let us know if you find anything else."

As Clo ended the call, the car was silent for a moment, the gravity of the situation thickening around them.

Grimshaw was the first to break the silence, his voice low but serious. "Paul Reid knew. He either ignored what was happening or let it continue. And Molly? She had nowhere to turn."

Clo's eyes flashed with anger. "This woman crossed boundaries, and Molly's dad just looked the other way. No wonder she wanted to get away."

Grimshaw's gaze hardened, the pieces falling into place in his mind. "What if it's more than just looking the other way?"

Clo frowned, trying to catch up with Grimshaw's line of thinking. "More than what?"

Grimshaw's voice was steady but charged with urgency. "We've got Molly's father acting suspiciously disappearing for hours with his phone off. Then we've got this mystery woman, manipulating Molly, making her uncomfortable. And now DarkSeraphim—someone who knows how to manipulate and control—swoops in at the perfect time, offering Molly an escape."

Clo's brow furrowed as she pieced together Grimshaw's suggestion. "You think they're connected? Paul, the woman, and DarkSeraphim?"

Grimshaw nodded slowly, his expression grim. "It's possible. What if DarkSeraphim isn't just some random online predator? What if they've been working with—or are connected to—Paul or this woman?"

Clo's breath hitched at the thought. "Are you saying Paul Reid might be involved with DarkSeraphim? Using them to lure Molly back or manipulate her further?"

Grimshaw shook his head, though the possibility clearly unsettled him. "Not necessarily. But maybe this woman—whoever she is—has some connection to DarkSeraphim. Maybe she introduced Molly to them, or maybe they're working together."

"Or maybe this woman is DarkSeraphim?" Suggest Clo

Clo's face paled as the implications sank in. "If Paul Reid knows this woman has been manipulating Molly and he's involved... that changes everything. It means Molly's been betrayed by the very people who are supposed to protect her."

Grimshaw's voice remained steady but cold. "Exactly. Molly would have felt completely trapped. With nowhere to turn, DarkSeraphim offering her an escape would be irresistible."

Clo's heart started to sink the enormity of the situation sinking in. "But why? What would they gain from pulling Molly in like this?"

Grimshaw thought for a moment, his gaze distant as he connected the dots. "Control. If Paul and this woman want to manipulate Molly—whether for money, power, or some other twisted reason—DarkSeraphim is the perfect tool to push her away from everyone else and into their hands."

The case had just taken a much darker turn. If Grimshaw was right, Molly's situation was far more dangerous than they had initially realised. "We need to find Molly," Clo said, her voice firm and filled with determination. "Before DarkSeraphim—or whoever's pulling the strings—takes her completely."

Grimshaw nodded, his jaw clenched. "And we need to figure out exactly how Paul Reid fits into all of this."

There was a long pause as both detectives processed the revelation. Clo clenched her fists, anger rising as she thought about Molly, manipulated by people she should have been able to trust. "If Paul's involved, this whole situation is worse than we thought. Molly's fear might be the key—if DarkSeraphim's feeding her paranoia, making her think she has no one left, she's more vulnerable than ever."

The clock was ticking but every second seemed to bring more questions than answers to the fore.

Chapter 12: Shadows at the Harbour

Molly's heart pounded in her chest as she made her way across the road and towards the harbour. The mid-day sun was high in the sky but Molly didn't register this, her mind was racing and she couldn't focus on any of the thoughts that were running through it.

"My dad's tracking me - that man and woman up ahead look like an odd couple - no one understands me – this phone is my only lifeline – the guy behind the counter in the coffee shop was friendly - why wasn't my mam wanting to help – no one sees me – I need to get to safety – why did I have to go to that stupid sleepover"

All of these thoughts were tripping over each other so fast that she couldn't pin them down and put them in order, flowing like water over the edge of a waterfall and crashing at the bottom so loud it was hard to focus

The only thing she could register in all of that was that DarkSeraphim's last message had been clear "Head to the harbour. Someone will meet you there. Someone I trust" Each step felt heavier than the last, the weight of her exhaustion and anxiety dragging her down. She entered the harbour and headed to the car park at the far side where she knew the sloping beach was.

As she neared the carpark, her heart lurched violently in her chest. Standing near the water, talking on a phone, was Lisa Stewart—one of her father's closest friends. The sight of her sent a cold, creeping chill down Molly's spine. She froze, her stomach twisting in knots, her mind flashing with memories she had tried to forget.

Molly's breath caught in her throat as the familiar sensation of discomfort flooded her mind. There was something about Lisa that had always unnerved her, something in the way her words were too personal, too intimate. Lisa had a habit of commenting on Molly's appearance, remarks that left her skin crawling. She had brushed it off at first, telling herself that she was being paranoid, that it was all in her head. But now, seeing Lisa here, at the harbour, all those buried suspicions rose to the surface with brutal clarity.

What is she doing here?

Panic surged through Molly, memories rushing back in a flood of unease. The uncomfortable way Lisa had looked at her, the way her casual words had felt too close, too knowing. Molly's instincts screamed at her to leave, to run, but she was rooted to the spot.

She's looking for me. She's working with my dad.

The realisation hit Molly like a punch to the gut. Lisa was here because of her father. They were working together to track her down, to take her back to the suffocating life she had fled. Molly's breath quickened, her heart hammering in her chest as panic set in. Her vision blurred as her mind spiralled out of control.

I can't go back. I won't go back. They're trying to take me.

Without thinking, Molly turned sharply, her footsteps quickening as she walked away from the harbour, her thoughts muddling together in a fog of fear. Her heart pounded so loudly it drowned out the distant sounds of the dockworkers and the sea breeze. Every face she passed blurred into one—a potential threat, an enemy. She glanced over her shoulder repeatedly, half-expecting to see Lisa following her, closing in like a predator.

Don't let them catch you. Keep moving. Don't stop.

Her legs trembled, her knees threatening to give way beneath her as she stumbled along the pavement. She ducked into a narrow alley behind the chip shop, leaning against a damp brick wall for support. Her breath came in ragged, shallow bursts as panic clawed at her chest. Her thoughts raced, a jumbled mess of fear and desperation. She was alone. No one understood—no one but DarkSeraphim. They were her only escape, her only chance.

In her blind panic, Molly had forgotten to check her phone. She didn't see the new message from DarkSeraphim that had arrived moments earlier.

Across town, DarkSeraphim sat in their car with their laptop open in front of them, frustration building with every minute that passed without a response from Molly. Their fingers drummed impatiently on the steering wheel, irritation bubbling just beneath the surface. The plan had been meticulously crafted—every step, every word calculated to pull Molly in. But now, Molly wasn't responding, and their control over the situation felt increasingly fragile.

They opened the chat with Molly, quickly typing another message. This time, they laced it with concern, masking their growing impatience with a veneer of kindness.

"Are you okay? Are you on your way? I've got someone I trust waiting for you. They'll keep you safe."

They hit send and stared at the screen, waiting. Nothing. The silence gnawed at them. Molly was fragile, and they had to tread carefully. If they pushed too hard, she might break away. But if they didn't push enough, she might slip out of their grasp entirely.

I can't lose her now. Not after everything.

Another minute passed, and still no reply. DarkSeraphim's fingers hovered over the keys, their frustration intensifying. Molly was supposed to be at the harbour by now where the car was waiting to pick her up. She had followed their instructions before, but something was wrong. They couldn't afford to lose control. Not now.

They typed another message, this time with a hint of urgency, their frustration bleeding into their words despite their best efforts to remain calm.

"Please let me know you're okay. I'm worried about you. My friend is waiting—don't keep them too long, you're so close to escaping the world that has you feeling so isolated"

The message sent, and DarkSeraphim clenched their jaw, trying to maintain composure. If Molly didn't respond soon, the entire plan could unravel.

Molly stumbled through the narrow alley, her breath coming in short, painful bursts. Her chest felt tight, the fear gnawing at her like a relentless animal. She had to get away—from Lisa, from the harbour, from everything. The cold wind whipped around her as she fled, her vision blurring as tears stung her eyes. Every sound felt like a threat, every passerby across the alley a potential spy sent by her father.

They're going to find me. They're going to drag me back.

Molly's hands shook so violently that she had to shove them into her pockets just to keep from losing her grip on reality. She was so consumed by fear that she barely registered the buzzing of her phone in her pocket. She was running on pure adrenaline now, her legs barely supporting her as she stumbled through the streets.

Only DarkSeraphim understands. Only they can help me.

Finally, after what felt like hours of running although only a couple of minutes had passed by, Molly slowed down, her breath coming in ragged gasps. She pulled out her phone, her hands still trembling as she blinked, trying to focus on the screen. Several messages from DarkSeraphim lit up her notifications.

DarkSeraphim: Please let me know you're okay. I'm worried about you.

Molly's chest tightened. Worried about me? DarkSeraphim had never said that before. The thought of them abandoning her, of being truly alone, sent a fresh wave of panic coursing through her veins. What if they give up on me? What if they leave me too? DarkSeraphim was the only one who had ever cared about her. They were the only ones who truly understood her. She couldn't lose them. Not now. Not ever.

Her fingers flew across the screen, her desperation spilling into her message:

"I'm sorry. As I got to the harbour. I saw someone—Lisa, one of my dad's friends. She used to make me feel uncomfortable. I'm scared she's looking for me. I didn't know what to do."

She hit send, her heart racing as she waited for DarkSeraphim's response.

DarkSeraphim read Molly's message quickly, a mixture of frustration and relief flooding through them. Molly had finally responded. That was all that mattered. Lisa was irrelevant, a minor irritation that could have ruined it all. What mattered now was pulling Molly back in, keeping her tethered to the carefully constructed narrative they had built.

They quickly typed a response, keeping their tone soft and reassuring, carefully nurturing Molly's trust.

"It's okay, Molly. I understand. I would've been scared too. But you're safe now. Keep moving away from her. We'll figure this out together."

They paused, considering their next move. Molly's fear was palpable, her vulnerability raw. She was scared, which made her dependent—exactly what DarkSeraphim needed. They had to keep her close, keep her trust alive. As they directed Molly they messaged the other car "Change of plan get to the hilltop carpark where I am now! She is coming there"

Molly's fingers trembled as she read DarkSeraphim's message. Keep moving. But where? Where could she go? Her mind spun with uncertainty, her panic still gripping her chest like a vice. She had to trust them. They were the only ones who understood. The only ones who had ever tried to help her.

Her feet moved automatically as she followed DarkSeraphim's guidance, heading toward the hilltop car park, a quiet spot on the outskirts of Seaham that overlooked the town. Her thoughts were a blur, replaying the image of Lisa at the harbour, the unsettling memories of her words, her touch.

As Molly approached the car park, she spotted a figure standing near a dark car at the far end. The person was dressed in a style similar to hers—dark clothes, heavy boots. They smiled warmly as she got closer, a smile that made her feel, if only for a moment like she was safe.

"Let me guess," the person said, their voice low and soothing. "Molly, right? DS sent me. You're safe now."

They gestured toward the car. "We've got a place for you. Let's get you out of here."

For the first time in what felt like days, Molly exhaled a shaky breath of relief. This is it. DarkSeraphim kept their promise. She nodded silently, climbing into the passenger seat. As the door clicked shut, her anxiety began to ebb, the tension loosening its grip. She felt safer now, knowing she was finally escaping.

Back in town, Grimshaw and Clo sat in their car at the harbour after looking around and not seeing Molly, frustration building as they struggled to piece together Molly's movements. Clo's phone rang suddenly, breaking the tense silence—it was the barista from the café they had visited earlier.

"I just saw that girl you were asking about—Molly, right? She was heading toward the hilltop car park," the barista said, his voice hurried.

Clo's eyes widened as she relayed the information to Grimshaw. "She's headed toward the hilltop car park," Clo said, urgency filling her voice. "Let's go. We might still catch her."

They sped toward the car park, tension thick in the air between them. Clo's knuckles were white on the steering wheel as they raced through the narrow streets of Seaham. Grimshaw sat rigid, his eyes scanning the road ahead, hoping to catch sight of Molly before it was too late.

They raced into the car park and turned to the left-hand side of the car park "There!" Clo shouted, pointing as they reached the end of the car park.

A black saloon was pulling out onto the road, its wheels kicking up dust as it accelerated. Grimshaw's heart sank as he caught a glimpse of Molly in the passenger seat, her face turned away as the car sped off. Just as they entered the car park, the saloon disappeared around the bend.

"That's her!" Grimshaw slammed his fist against the dashboard, frustration boiling over. "That's Molly!"

Clo quickly braked, swerving the car into a nearby space to avoid blocking the exit. Grimshaw's sharp eyes caught the number plate of the departing car just in time.

"CF28 RBU," Grim muttered under his breath, grabbing his radio. "Control, we need an all-points bulletin on a black saloon, registration CF28 RBU. It just left the hilltop car park in Seaham, heading east back towards Seaham centre. We need ANPR cameras on it now."

Clo had barely started to turn the car around when a silver hatchback suddenly pulled out from one of the nearby spaces, moving at an agonisingly slow pace. The hatchback crept across the car park, deliberately blocking their path. Clo's hands tightened on the wheel, her knuckles white with frustration.

"COME ON, COME ON!" she muttered through clenched teeth, hitting the horn in frustration.

The driver of the silver hatchback barely glanced back, their expression unreadable, but Grimshaw's sharp gaze caught something in the rearview mirror—was it a slight smirk, as though they knew exactly what they were doing?

"Feels like they're stalling us," Grimshaw muttered, his jaw tightening. His suspicion intensified when the hatchback continued its sluggish crawl, ensuring Grim and Clo couldn't follow Molly's car.

Clo honked again, her foot tapping impatiently against the accelerator. "We're losing her," she hissed, watching as the black saloon grew smaller in the distance.

Grimshaw's eyes narrowed. "They're doing this on purpose. They know we're chasing Molly."

Seconds stretched into an eternity as the silver hatchback finally cleared the exit, pulling off in the opposite direction. By the time Clo accelerated, Molly's car was already gone, disappearing along the country road, a road that ultimately led to the A19.

"Damn it!" Clo growled, slamming her fist against the steering wheel before speeding off in the direction the saloon had gone.

Grimshaw was already on the radio, his voice tight with urgency. "Control, we need live tracking on that vehicle's registration. ANPR cameras—everywhere. Get eyes on it. We cannot lose that car."

As they pulled out of the car park and sped after the vehicle, Grimshaw's mind raced. They had come so close, but DarkSeraphim's plan had bought them precious minutes—and Molly was now in the hands of someone they couldn't yet identify.

Chapter 13: Ghosts in the Rearview

Clo gripped the steering wheel with white-knuckled intensity as they sped through the narrow streets of Seaham, the car's tyres screeching as they took sharp turns. The world outside the car became a blur of colours, the shapes of buildings and people melting into a dizzying rush. Next to her, Grimshaw sat silent, his eyes scanning the road ahead, every car that passed, and every sign that pointed toward their target. The atmosphere in the car was thick—dense with the kind of urgency that clung to their skin, wrapping around their every wordless exchange.

The roar of the engine filled the space between them, drowning out their thoughts but doing nothing to ease the tension that had been brewing between them since the call about Molly. The stakes had never felt higher, the frustration and fear of being one step behind gnawing at them both. This wasn't just a chase—it was personal, in ways neither of them could quite articulate. Yet, it was there, lingering in the space between their breaths.

As they drove past the harbour and out the other side of Seaham they could see up ahead like a pink prick at the crest of the hill the car they had seen Molly in, however as Grimshaw focused and felt we were going to catch them he suddenly felt his body fly forward and felt the seatbelt dig into him as Clo had slammed on the breaks [brakes], as he came back to his immediate surroundings he realised why. There were road works blocking one of the lanes where there was a new housing estate being built and the lights for their side were on red as cars from the other side were already heading towards them; the fear of loss and disappointment filled him up.

Clo tapped her fingers nervously against the steering wheel while she waited for the cars to clear so she could continue the chase, her mind spinning with the memories she had spent years trying to bury. There was something about this case that was becoming too familiar, something about Molly's situation that was pulling at her own scars—the kind that never fully healed, no matter how much time passed.

She glanced sideways at Grimshaw, his face a mask of control, but beneath it, she sensed the same turbulence. Although they had only worked together for such a short space of time she started to notice the cracks, even if Grimshaw was skilled at keeping them hidden. Clo wondered what demons he was wrestling with in the silence, what ghosts were haunting him just as her own past clawed at her mind.

"I get it now," she said suddenly, her voice cutting through the tension.

Grimshaw didn't turn, his eyes still fixed on the road, but she saw the slight flicker of acknowledgement in his expression. "Get what?"

"This case," she continued, her voice quieter now, more introspective. "It's hitting home for you, isn't it? I've seen that look on your face before. It's the same one I get when I think about... my past."

Grimshaw's grip on the armrest tightened, his jaw clenching as her words settled between them. He wasn't one for personal conversations, especially not on the job, but something about this case—the missing girl, the manipulation, the chase—it was starting to unravel the walls he'd built around himself.

"There was a case," Grimshaw said, his voice low, measured. "A few years back. A young girl, the same age as Molly, went missing in the middle of the night." He paused, his eyes narrowing as if the memory played out in front of him, vivid and painful. "We were closing in on her, thought we had found her. But we didn't. We were too late. Found her a week later... and well that sort of image never leaves you."

Clo winced, feeling the weight of his words settles in the pit of her stomach. She didn't need more details. The pain in Grimshaw's voice was enough.

"That's why you push so hard," she said softly, understanding now. "You're trying to make up for it."

Grimshaw gave a curt nod, his voice tightening. "This case feels too much like that one. Same pattern. Same helplessness. It feels like we're always one step behind."

Clo's heart clenched at his words. She knew what it was like to be haunted by the past, to carry the kind of guilt that gnaws at you, even in your sleep. The image of her sister flashed in her mind—the face she'd avoided thinking about for so long. She didn't talk about her family, not to anyone, but something about this case, about Grimshaw's words, cracked something open in her.

"You're not the only one haunted, Grim," she said quietly, her voice barely audible over the hum of the engine. "My sister... she killed my mum. I was just a kid. I didn't see it coming. Didn't stop it."

For the first time, Grimshaw's eyes flicked toward her, surprise flickering in his usually impassive gaze. With Molly's life hanging in the balance, the words spilt out before she could stop them.

"It's why I joined the force," she continued, her voice stronger now. "I thought maybe I could stop other families from falling apart. Maybe I could fix something."

Grimshaw nodded, understanding etched into his expression. "We all have our ghosts."

The weight of their shared pasts hung heavy in the car, but for the first time, it didn't feel like a barrier between them. Instead, it connected them—two detectives chasing redemption, trying to outrun the ghosts of their own failures.

Meanwhile, DarkSeraphim was driving alone in a silver saloon, their hands steady on the wheel. The car hummed quietly beneath them, the steady rhythm of the engine a calming contrast to the chaos swirling in their mind. They were always calculating, always planning, and everything had fallen into place, maybe not as perfect as they had planned but it had fallen into place all the same.

DarkSeraphim glanced briefly at the dashboard before accessing the car's Bluetooth system, scrolling through their contacts until they found the one they were looking for. They pressed dial, waiting as the call connected. The voice on the other end answered quickly, quiet but expectant.

"It's me," DarkSeraphim said, their voice calm, measured, as always. "Molly's on her way. She shouldn't be long now."

There was a brief pause on the other end, followed by a murmured response.

"Make sure she's comfortable," DarkSeraphim continued. "She's been through a lot, so let her shower and freshen up when she gets there. Give her something to eat—nothing too heavy. She'll be tense."

Another pause and DarkSeraphim's lips curved into a faint smile as they added, almost affectionately, "Make her feel at home. I'll be there soon. Just one more stop to make."

With that, they ended the call, a sense of satisfaction settling over them. Everything was going according to plan. Molly was falling deeper into their hands, and by the end of the night, they would have complete control.

Back in the car, Grimshaw's phone buzzed with an incoming update from the station. He glanced at the screen, his expression tightening as he quickly read the message. "The ANPR cameras picked up the car," he said, his voice taut with urgency. "It left the A19 at the A690 turn-off, heading toward Houghton-le-Spring."

Clo's pulse quickened as she adjusted the route, taking the exit toward the A690. "We're close," she said, her focus narrowing as she pushed the car harder. "We can still catch them."

Grimshaw's eyes remained fixed on the road ahead, his voice low. "We're close, but they're smart. If we lose them now, we might not pick up the trail again."

Clo nodded grimly, her grip tightening on the wheel. She wasn't going to lose Molly. Not now. Not when they were this close. The road ahead stretched out, long and winding, but determination fuelled every movement, every turn. They had both lost too much already—too many cases gone wrong, too many regrets. But Molly… Molly still had a chance.

"We won't lose her," Clo said, her voice firm with resolve. "Not this time."

Grimshaw glanced at her, his eyes softening for a brief moment. He didn't say anything, but the shared understanding between them was palpable. They were in this together, and they weren't going to let Molly slip through their fingers.

Meanwhile, in the black car, Molly's stomach churned with a growing sense of unease. The driver, Alan, had introduced himself with a calm smile, his voice steady as he reassured her that everything was going to be fine. But something about the situation didn't sit right with her. The farther they drove, the more isolated the surroundings became. The narrow country lane they had turned onto was flanked by tall hedgerows, and the bustling streets of Seaham felt like a distant memory.

Molly glanced nervously at Alan, who drove with smooth precision, his hands steady on the wheel. He hadn't said much since they'd left the town behind, but his presence was unsettling in its calmness. Molly's mind raced with conflicting thoughts. DarkSeraphim had promised her safety and had assured her that she could trust them. But now, as they approached a large, isolated farmhouse, Molly couldn't shake the feeling that something was wrong.

The farmhouse loomed ahead, its stone walls worn but strong, the windows glowing faintly with light. It looked idyllic, almost serene, but the stillness of the place made Molly's heart race. She had seen scenes like this before—in TV shows, in movies—where the endings were never good.

"Is this where you live?" Molly asked hesitantly, her voice small in the quiet of the car.

Alan shook his head, his smile never faltering. "No, Molly. This is just a safe place for tonight. Somewhere quiet, away from everything. Tomorrow, we'll take you to where you'll be living."

Molly nodded slowly, trying to take in his words, but a flicker of panic stirred in her gut. The farmhouse looked safe enough, quiet and secluded like they had promised, but her thoughts betrayed her. Was this really safe? Or had she walked into something far more dangerous?

As the car pulled up to the front of the farmhouse, Molly's doubts gnawed at her. She had come this far, trusting DarkSeraphim every step of the way. But now, faced with the reality of this isolated place, her mind couldn't stop racing. She wanted to believe she was safe. She needed to. But the silence was too thick, too still.

Was this her escape? Or had she just walked into a trap?

Back on the A690, Grimshaw and Clo raced through the night, the blue lights of their car reflecting off the dark road as they tore through the countryside. The ANPR cameras had last picked up Molly's car just before Sherburn Village, but now the trail had gone cold. Every second felt like an eternity, and Clo's frustration mounted as they navigated the narrow roads.

"Come on," Grimshaw muttered under his breath, his eyes scanning the dark countryside, willing the black car to reappear. "We're close."

The silence between them was heavy, both detectives fully aware of the race against time. Somewhere ahead, Molly was in danger, and with every passing second, the gap between them and their target widened.

"We have to find her, Grim," Clo said, her voice tight with determination.

Grimshaw gave a slight nod, his gaze hardening. "We will."

Chapter 14: Unveiling the New Family Web

DarkSeraphim parked the silver saloon outside the outlet shopping centre, the engine's hum fading into silence as their heartbeat pounded in their ears. They stared through the windshield, their thoughts spiralling in a whirlwind of anxiety. Everything had gone sideways since Saturday. What had begun as a carefully orchestrated plan to manipulate Molly had suddenly unravelled, threatening to expose everything. Today's events—the chaos at the harbour and Molly's panic—had nearly destroyed all they had worked for.

They clenched their fists, trying to calm the rising panic before shoving their hands into their coat pockets. As they crossed the car park, the usual buzz of distant traffic and chattering shoppers felt muffled, drowned out by the roar of DarkSeraphim's racing thoughts. Every step toward the supermarket café felt like walking through thick mud, their feet heavy, weighed down by the anxiety of the upcoming meeting. They had been summoned here, and it wasn't for a casual conversation. No, this was going to be brutal.

The automatic doors slid open with a soft whoosh, the rush of warm air inside doing nothing to soothe DarkSeraphim's nerves. The supermarket bustled with life—trolleys rattling down aisles, families chattering, and the high-pitched beep of checkout scanners filling the space. But none of it mattered. DarkSeraphim had only one destination: the café tucked away in the back corner, where an entirely different atmosphere awaited.

As they approached, their thoughts raced. Molly had almost slipped through their fingers at the harbour. Saturday's cancelled meet-up had shaken Molly badly, and while DarkSeraphim had been carefully working to rebuild trust, today's events had brought everything to the verge of crashing down again. Molly's unexpected arrival in Seaham had been an unwelcome surprise, but it was the woman from Molly's past—Lisa Stewart—who had nearly ruined everything.

DarkSeraphim's heart pounded as the café came into view. The figure waiting in the far corner was unmistakable. She sat tall, her fingers drumming lightly against a ceramic mug, her gaze piercing through the space between them. DarkSeraphim swallowed hard, forcing their feet forward, though every instinct screamed to turn and run. There was no avoiding this. Survival hinged on this meeting.

The cold sweat trickling down the back of DarkSeraphim's neck intensified as they neared the table. Their mind raced, struggling to piece together the right words, to offer an explanation that might diffuse the volatile storm gathering in her eyes.

Finally, they reached the table and slid into the seat across from her, avoiding eye contact as long as possible. But she didn't let them off easily. Her gaze was sharp, cutting through the silence like a blade, her presence suffocating. DarkSeraphim opened their mouth to speak, but she beat them to it.

"Explain. Now," she demanded, her voice low, but its edge sharper than broken glass.

DarkSeraphim swallowed the lump in their throat, the words catching before they managed to reply. "I didn't know Molly was going to be in Seaham," they began, trying to maintain a steady tone. "Getting her to the harbour wasn't part of the plan. I was still working to arrange a new meet-up after Saturday's cancellation, but things have been tense. She's been paranoid, on edge. And when she saw you..."

Lisa Stewart's eyes narrowed, and her fingers drummed more deliberately against the mug. "You think I don't know that? I saw her hurrying away" she hissed, her voice dangerously cold. "I was overseeing an important delivery at the harbour. Do you have any idea how delicate this situation is?"

DarkSeraphim stiffened, their pulse quickening. "It wasn't intentional. I was trying to get her to a safe spot before the police found her. I didn't know you'd still be there. The harbour was just... convenient."

Lisa's fingers stilled, her gaze darkening as she leaned in, her voice dropping to a chilling whisper. "Convenient? If Molly had put two and two together, it would've been over. For all of us."

The weight of Lisa's words pressed down on DarkSeraphim like a lead blanket. Her tone wasn't a warning—it was a death sentence, hanging precariously above their head, waiting to drop at the slightest mistake.

"I understand," DarkSeraphim replied quickly, their voice tight with fear. "I've been rebuilding her trust since Saturday. She's been scared—paranoid that her father is tracking her. I'm using that fear to keep her close, to bring her back under control."

Lisa leaned back in her chair, a cruel smile creeping across her lips. "Smart. Keep pushing that fear. The more terrified she is of her father, the easier it will be to control her."

DarkSeraphim nodded, feeling a small flicker of relief as the tension in Lisa's posture seemed to ease slightly. "She's completely reliant on the new phone now, she sees it as her only lifeline. The old one is gone—left behind at home."

Lisa's eyes gleamed with satisfaction, though her voice remained icy. "Good. That was a clever idea—leaving the phone for her to find. You suggested that didn't you?"

DarkSeraphim allowed themselves a brief moment of pride. "It had to feel like it was meant for her. The bow, the card with 'DS' on it—it had to feel like a gift, something she could trust."

Lisa's smile sharpened, but the approval was fleeting. Her expression hardened again, her voice dropping to a dangerous whisper. "But don't forget—Molly is essential to the plan. If you mess this up again, there will be consequences. Severe ones. You know how much he wants her."

DarkSeraphim's stomach twisted with fear, Lisa's words reverberating through their mind like the tolling of a death knell. One more mistake, and they would pay dearly for it.

"I won't let it happen again," DarkSeraphim promised, their voice barely above a whisper.

Lisa stood abruptly, her coat swishing as she adjusted it. "See that you don't," she said, her voice cold. "I expect an update soon. Molly is crucial to what comes next. We can't afford any more slip-ups."

With that, Lisa turned on her heel and strode out of the café, her presence leaving a cold, oppressive weight behind. DarkSeraphim remained seated, frozen in place as the gravity of the meeting settled in. Every word Lisa had spoken echoed in their mind, a constant reminder of how high the stakes had become. They couldn't afford to fail—not now. Molly had to be fully under their control, no more slip-ups, no more near misses. If Lisa's plan was going to succeed, DarkSeraphim had to be perfect.

But perfection, as DarkSeraphim knew all too well, wasn't easy to achieve.

Molly hesitated at the door of the old farmhouse, the rumble of the black car's engine fading behind her as she turned to see it driving away back up the track. The sun had begun to dip below the horizon, casting long shadows over the rolling hills and the aged stone walls of the house. It was quiet, eerily so, with only the faint rustle of leaves carried by the evening breeze. Molly's nerves twisted inside her, but she pushed the fear down as best she could. DarkSeraphim had assured her this place was safe, that this was where she would find the family she had been searching for. She wanted—needed—to believe that.

Before she could knock, the door swung open, revealing a young woman with a warm, inviting smile. She looked to be in her late twenties, with dark hair pulled loosely back and sharp but kind eyes that swept over Molly's dishevelled appearance without judgment.

"You must be Molly," the woman said, her voice soothing. "I'm Abbie. It's so good to finally meet you. Come in—you're safe now."

Molly felt some of the tension ease from her shoulders at the sound of Abbie's voice, the warmth in her tone melting away some of the fear that had been building all day. She stepped inside, and Abbie shut the door behind her, the heavy wooden latch clicking into place with a sense of finality that Molly couldn't quite shake.

Abbie gently placed a hand on Molly's arm, guiding her through the hallway. The farmhouse's interior was cozy, far more inviting than Molly had expected. Warm wooden floors creaked beneath their feet, and soft lighting bathed the rooms in a golden glow. The faint smell of something baking in the oven added to the comforting atmosphere. For the first time in days, Molly allowed herself to take a deep breath.

"You don't have to worry anymore," Abbie said as they walked. "You're safe here. This is your new family now, and we're all so happy to have you."

Molly's heart fluttered at the word family. It had been so long since she had felt like she belonged anywhere. She glanced up at Abbie, her nervous energy still buzzing beneath the surface, but Abbie's gentle presence made it easier to relax. She had been so lost, so alone, but now—now, she wasn't. DarkSeraphim had found her, and they had given her this new family. Maybe, finally, she could feel at home.

Abbie led Molly up a flight of stairs, the wood creaking softly beneath their steps. She opened the door to a beautiful, light-filled bedroom. Soft pastel colours adorned the walls, and a large window overlooked the peaceful countryside towards a wood neatly placed at the end of the fields. In the centre of the room stood a plush bed, its white linens looking inviting after days of discomfort. A nightstand and wardrobe flanked the bed, and in the corner, a gleaming ensuite bathroom beckoned with its spotless tiled floor.

"This is your room," Abbie said with a smile, stepping back to let Molly take it all in. "I hope you like it. It's all yours now."

Molly stood in the doorway, her mouth slightly open in awe. She hadn't expected this—she had pictured something far more stark and uncomfortable. But this... this was a sanctuary. It was beautiful, and, and it was hers.

Abbie moved toward the ensuite, flipping on the light. "Why don't you take a shower? Freshen up. You've had a long day, and I'm sure you could use a break. Take your time. I'll go make you something to eat and bring it up here for you."

Molly's voice came out small, almost uncertain. "Thank you," she whispered.

Abbie gave her another warm smile before turning to leave. "I'll be back soon. Just make yourself at home, okay?"

As the door closed behind her, Molly stood frozen for a moment, staring at the luxurious room around her. It didn't feel real. Could she really be safe now? Could she really belong here? The questions buzzed in her mind, but the soft glow of the room and the promise of a hot shower lured her forward.

Molly stepped into the bathroom and turned on the shower, the sound of rushing water calming her frayed nerves. She stripped off her clothes, her fingers trembling slightly from the tension still coiled inside her. But as the warm water cascaded over her skin, she felt the day's anxiety slowly start to melt away.

For the first time in days, Molly felt like she could finally start to let her guard down. She was here now, with people who understood her. People who cared. This was the family she had been searching for, wasn't it?

As the steam rose around her, Molly closed her eyes, allowing herself to believe—even if just for a moment—that everything was going to be okay.

Blissfully unaware of the web being spun around her.

Chapter 15: The Trap Tightens

Downstairs in the farmhouse kitchen, Abbie hummed softly to herself as she prepared a tray of food for Molly. The smell of roasted chicken, herbs, and spices filled the air, blending with the earthy aroma that drifted in through the open window. The countryside, tranquil and still, seemed worlds away from the danger gathering inside the farmhouse walls. Abbie moved with practised ease, setting the meal and drink in place, ensuring that every element was perfect.

The final touch—her secret ingredient—was slipped into the meal with the precision of someone who had done this many times before. It wasn't much, just enough to dull Molly's senses, to make her compliant. Too much and it would arouse suspicion, but the right amount would leave her vulnerable, confused, and easily controlled.

Abbie glanced at the stairs, her lips curling into a satisfied smile. Everything was going exactly as planned. Soon, Molly would be theirs to mould, her mind too fogged to resist. DarkSeraphim's plan was unfolding perfectly.

Just as Abbie finished preparing the tray, her phone buzzed on the counter. She wiped her hands on a towel, picking it up, and the familiar number flashing on the screen made her stomach tighten. She swiped to answer, her voice sharper than usual. "Yes?"

DarkSeraphim's voice came through, cool and calculated as always, though there was an unmistakable tension simmering beneath the surface. "How's it going with our new guest?"

Abbie's gaze flicked toward the stairs again, her tone softening. "She's in the shower now. I'm fixing up the usual for her."

"Good," DarkSeraphim replied, satisfaction creeping into their voice. "It's important Molly feels safe—for now. But we need to make sure she's fully compliant when the time comes."

"She will be," Abbie assured, though a hint of tension lingered in her voice. "But listen—if there's going to be more like her, I'm going to need more of this. My supplies are running low."

There was a pause on the other end, a brief hesitation before DarkSeraphim responded. "Understood. I'll have Alan arrange a collection for you."

Abbie nodded, her tension easing slightly. "And her phone?" she asked.

DarkSeraphim's voice turned colder, more focused. "You need to get rid of it, Quietly, Separate her from it. Alan will handle the rest when he arrives."

As the call ended, Abbie pocketed her phone, glancing at the tray with a tight smile. Everything was going as planned. Molly wouldn't suspect a thing. The drugs mixed into the food would take effect soon after she ate, and by then, it would be too late for her to fight back. Molly had no idea how far she was sinking into their trap.

Upstairs, Molly had finished her shower, wrapping herself in a soft towel. The steam from the bathroom swirled around her, clinging to the air like a warm embrace, but the tension in her chest refused to ease. The warmth of the shower had relaxed her muscles, but her mind was still buzzing with unease. The farmhouse was so quiet, so peaceful—too peaceful.

Molly stood in front of the mirror, watching the droplets of water trail down her skin, her reflection staring back at her with wide, anxious eyes. She wanted to believe that everything was okay, that this place was as safe as it seemed. But something gnawed at the back of her mind, a voice whispering that things weren't as perfect as they appeared.

Where's my phone?

The thought hit her like a bolt of lightning, sending a fresh wave of panic surging through her. She hadn't seen it since she arrived at the farmhouse. She had been so overwhelmed by the relief of finding a safe place, of finally escaping, that she hadn't even thought to check for it. Now, though, the absence of her phone felt like a gaping hole in her safety net.

Molly's heart began to race as she quickly searched through her bag, her towel slipping slightly as she frantically rifled through her belongings. Nothing. Her phone was gone. Panic clawed at her throat, tightening its grip as her thoughts spiralled. Had she left it in the car? Had she dropped it somewhere?

Just as she was about to leave the room and search the house, there was a soft knock on the door. Abbie stepped inside, balancing the tray of food in her hands, her smile as warm as ever.

"Here we go," Abbie said brightly, setting the tray on the bedside table. "hope your hungry."

Molly tried to force a smile, but the growing panic about her phone twisted her stomach into knots. "Actually... have you seen my phone? I can't seem to find it."

Abbie's expression didn't falter for a second. She let out a light laugh, waving a hand dismissively. "Oh, I bet you left it in Alan's car. Don't worry, I'll ask him to check when he gets back. Just relax for now. You need to eat."

Molly hesitated, but the mention of her phone being safe—even temporarily out of reach—calmed her nerves slightly. If it was with Alan, she could get it back later. Her stomach growled audibly, reminding her of how long it had been since she last ate.

"Thanks," she mumbled, trying to push her concerns aside as she sat on the edge of the bed, eyeing the food. The roasted chicken looked delicious, its golden skin glistening in the soft light of the room, and the smell was enough to make her mouth water. Without thinking, she dug in, the tender meat practically melting in her mouth.

She barely noticed the faint bitterness in the sauce, masked by the rich flavours of the herbs and spices. Her hunger overpowered her caution, and she gulped down the juice in one swift motion.

Abbie watched her with quiet satisfaction, standing a few steps away from the bed. "Take your time," she said, her voice soothing. "You're safe here."

Molly nodded, too focused on quelling her hunger to respond. Her muscles relaxed as the meal settled in her stomach, the warmth of the food spreading through her body. But soon, a heaviness began to creep in—slowly at first, then more rapidly.

Why am I so tired?

Molly blinked, her vision blurring as she tried to focus on Abbie. The edges of her sight softened, and her thoughts began to slow as if her mind were moving through molasses. "I... feel... strange..." she mumbled, her voice weak and distant.

Abbie's smile never wavered as she watched Molly's limbs grow heavy, her body sinking into the bed. Within moments, Molly was unconscious, her world fading to black.

Half an hour later, a sleek silver saloon pulled up silently in front of the farmhouse, its dark exterior blending into the landscape as the night began to settle in. The driver's door opened, and DarkSeraphim stepped out, their movements graceful and deliberate. The air was cool, the only sound was the faint rustle of leaves and the distant call of night birds as they approached the house.

Inside, the farmhouse was quiet. DarkSeraphim's footsteps were soft and measured as they crossed the threshold and moved through the living room, noting Abbie's absence. They climbed the stairs, their steps even, their mind already focused on the next phase of the plan.

At the top of the stairs, Abbie stood by the bedroom door, her face a picture of calm. As DarkSeraphim approached, she stepped aside, nodding toward the bed where Molly lay, her chest rising and falling softly beneath the towel wrapped around her.

"She's out cold," Abbie said in a low voice, her eyes flicking toward DarkSeraphim. "She ate it all."

DarkSeraphim moved to the edge of the bed, their gaze falling on Molly's unconscious form. For a moment, they stood still, watching her with a mixture of cold calculation and something darker, something more primal. The sight of Molly, so vulnerable, stirred something inside them—something they had kept buried for a long time.

Slowly, they reached out, their fingers brushing lightly over Molly's bare shoulder. The touch was delicate, almost reverent, but it sent a thrill through DarkSeraphim that they hadn't anticipated. Molly would have recoiled if she were awake, but now, under the influence of the drugs, she was completely unaware.

Satisfied, DarkSeraphim reached into their coat pocket, pulling out a syringe filled with a clear liquid. The sedative. Molly needed to be kept under for the next stage of the plan, and this would ensure that she remained docile and compliant.

Without hesitation, DarkSeraphim pressed the needle into Molly's skin, injecting her swiftly. Molly didn't stir, her body already slipping further into an unnatural stillness.

DarkSeraphim watched her for a moment longer, their gaze unreadable. Molly was a tool, a piece in a much larger puzzle. But standing over her now, they couldn't deny the power they felt. Molly was completely at their mercy, and the control they had over her was intoxicating.

"She'll be under for hours," DarkSeraphim muttered to Abbie, who stood nervously in the doorway.

Abbie swallowed, her eyes flicking between Molly and DarkSeraphim. "And the phone?"

DarkSeraphim smiled, slipping the empty syringe back into their pocket. "Alan will deal with it. It's gone."

With one last glance at Molly, DarkSeraphim straightened and turned to Abbie. "We need to move quickly. Molly's crucial for what's coming. No mistakes."

Abbie gave a small, tight smile. "No mistakes."

As DarkSeraphim stepped past her and headed back downstairs, Abbie lingered by the doorway, her gaze fixed on Molly's unconscious form. Everything was falling into place.

Meanwhile, parked on the side of a narrow country road, Grim and Clo sat in tense silence. The countryside lane stretched out ahead of them, the last remnants of daylight fading into dusk. Clo gripped the steering wheel, her knuckles white, frustration etched across her face. Beside her, Grim sat silent, his jaw clenched as he stared out the window, deep in thought.

They had lost Molly. The black saloon she had been whisked away in had disappeared from sight, and the weight of that failure gnawed at both of them.

"Damn it," Clo muttered, breaking the heavy silence. "We were so close. So damn close."

Grim didn't respond immediately, his jaw tight as he replayed the scene in his mind—the moment they saw Molly in the back of the car, helpless to stop it from speeding away. It left a bitter taste in his mouth, a frustration he hadn't felt in a long time.

"We couldn't have known," he said finally, his voice low. "It was too fast, too well-timed. They knew what they were doing."

Clo shook her head, unwilling to let it go. "She's out there now, Grim. God knows where, and she doesn't even know what she's walking into. She thinks she's safe with them, but we both know—" She couldn't finish the sentence, the weight of what Molly was facing too heavy to voice aloud.

Grim rubbed a hand over his face, feeling the burden of responsibility pressing down on him. Molly was vulnerable, and they had let her slip away.

"She's not gone yet," Grim said, forcing a note of determination into his voice. "We've got ANPR tracking the car. We'll pick up the trail again. But we need to act fast—DarkSeraphim has her now, and they won't waste time."

Clo let out a breath, nodding. "She's in real danger, Grim. She thinks DarkSeraphim is the only one who understands her. She's isolated—completely cut off from anyone who cares."

Grim frowned, his mind racing through everything they knew about DarkSeraphim. "If they're smart—and they've been two steps ahead so far—they'll have separated her from her phone by now."

Clo's expression was grim but resolute. "We need to find her, Grim. Before they do something, we can't undo."

Chapter 16: Quiet Reflections, Growing Doubts

Grimshaw sat silently in the passenger seat of the parked car, staring out at the darkening countryside. The low hum of distant traffic from the A690 was the only sound that pierced the otherwise quiet evening. The road ahead stretched out like a long, endless thread, and the quiet felt both oppressive and suffocating. His fingers drummed absently on his leg, the weight of everything pressing down on his chest like a heavy stone.

Next to him, Clo sat gripping the steering wheel, her own thoughts far from the empty road. She could feel the tension radiating off Grimshaw, the familiar storm of guilt and doubt that clung to him like a 1980's Spandex suit. The silence between them was thick, the kind that spoke volumes even though neither of them had said a word in the last ten minutes.

They were waiting for backup from Durham police, but the stillness that hung over them wasn't just about the delay. It was about what lay beneath the surface—what had been simmering ever since Molly slipped away from them in the car park. Grim's failure to stop her. Clo's helplessness in that split second when everything had gone wrong.

For Grimshaw, the silence was a reminder of past failures, a haunting echo of a case that still gnawed at him. His mind wandered back to a year ago when another young girl had disappeared under eerily similar circumstances. They had been close, so close to finding her, tracking her every move right up until the moment she vanished without a trace. Grimshaw had failed then, and that failure had never left him. It was always there, lurking in the back of his mind, a constant reminder of the lives he couldn't save.

And now, Molly was slipping through his fingers too.

"We lost her," Grimshaw said quietly, his voice rough with frustration. "Just like before."

Clo glanced at him, sensing the weight behind his words. She had heard Grimshaw briefly speak about one of his old cases earlier, She felt she knew how deeply it had scarred him. She also knew what it felt like to carry that kind of guilt.

"It's not over yet, Grim," she replied, trying to inject some hope into the conversation. But even she felt the cold grip of doubt tightening around her. Grimshaw wasn't the only one haunted by his past. Clo had her own demons, and this case was stirring them up in ways she hadn't expected.

Grim shook his head, staring out at the darkening sky. "I can't let her slip away like before, Not again."

The resignation in his voice made Clo's heart clench. She stayed silent for a moment, her thoughts drifting to her own past, the tragedy that had shaped her life—the murder of her mother at the hands of her twin sister. That pain was always there, lurking just beneath the surface, a constant reminder of how quickly life could spiral out of control. Clo had used her work to push the pain aside, to distract herself from the guilt that still haunted her. But cases like Molly's brought everything rushing back.

"This case…" Clo began, her voice soft. "It feels different, but in a way, it doesn't. Like Molly's caught in something bigger than she realises. Just like I was."

Grimshaw glanced at her, sensing the shift in her tone. "You mean with your sister?", Grimshaw had a brief understanding of what had happened as he had looked into her record the previous night, he always wanted to know as much as he could about a partner. [she already told him in ch.13]

Clo nodded, her jaw tightening, she didn't think about how he knew. "Yeah. You can be close to someone, trust them completely, and never see the danger until it's too late. I just hope we're not too late for Molly."

Grim didn't respond right away, but he understood. They were both haunted by their pasts, their regrets shaping the way they approached every case, and every decision. But this case—it felt personal in ways neither of them could fully explain.

Across the fields not too distant from where Grimshaw and Clo sat embroiled in thoughts about their own past, Paul Reid sat alone in his study, nursing a glass of whiskey in one hand and staring at the blank page in front of him. The paper, once meant to carry his confession, was untouched, save for a few scribbled-out lines he had tried—and failed—to write. His hands trembled as he lifted the glass to his lips, the amber liquid burning as it slid down his throat. The alcohol did little to dull the gnawing guilt that had been eating away at him for months.

Paul had been living a lie. It had all started with Lisa. The affair had been his first mistake, but it wasn't his last. Lisa had been a colleague and a trusted friend. For a while, Paul had convinced himself that the affair had been mutual, an escape from the monotony of his life. But everything had fallen apart when DarkSeraphim entered the picture.

DarkSeraphim had found out about the affair. Somehow, they had discovered the truth and started blackmailing him. At first, it was small things—money, information—but then it escalated. The demands became more sinister and more dangerous, and now they wanted Molly.

Paul stared down at the blank page in front of him, his heart heavy with guilt and regret. He had tried to resist DarkSeraphim's demands. He had tried to protect Molly, to find a way out of this nightmare, but the noose around his neck had only tightened. DarkSeraphim threatened to expose everything—to destroy his career, his reputation, and his family. He had no choice but to comply.

And Lisa... Lisa had known. She had played him like a puppet, using his fear and guilt to control him. Paul had thought, for a time, that Lisa had been manipulated too, that she was as much a victim of DarkSeraphim as he was. But now, he wasn't so sure. Lisa had always been in control, always one step ahead. Was she working with DarkSeraphim? Or was she just another pawn?

Paul no longer knew what to believe.

His phone buzzed on the desk, a sharp reminder of the hell he had created for himself. The message was from the same unknown number that had been tormenting him for weeks.

"You know what we need. Molly is the price you have to pay. You don't have a choice."

Paul gripped the phone tightly, his knuckles white as his thoughts churned. Anger, guilt, and an overwhelming sense of dread consumed him. He wanted to protect Molly, to find some way to save her, but how could he? He had already damned her.

He poured another glass of whiskey and stared at the blank page in front of him. He had thought about taking his own life, about leaving a confession behind to explain everything to his wife about Lisa and Molly and everything. Maybe, just maybe, it would save her. But each time he picked up the pen, the words refused to come. He couldn't leave her to face this alone. Not after everything he had done.

The silence of the room was suffocating, pressing down on him from all sides as the weight of his sins threatened to crush him.

As DarkSeraphim drove down the narrow country roads, their mind replayed the day's events over and over. Everything had been going according to plan—until today. Molly was supposed to be under their control, safely hidden away at the farmhouse days ago. But something about how things had unfolded gnawed at DarkSeraphim's confidence.

It wasn't the plan itself. The plan was solid. Molly had been lured in, and manipulated perfectly, just as they had done with so many others before her. The drugs had worked, and Molly was now tucked away, compliant and vulnerable.

But it had been too close.

Their mind kept returning to the moment in Seaham, in that coffee shop. Molly had been right there, walking past, and they hadn't noticed her. How had that happened? DarkSeraphim prided themselves on control, on always being one step ahead, but they had failed.

And then there was Grimshaw, they knew now who had held the door open for them at the coffee shop *(how did they know?)*

DarkSeraphim could still picture him—holding the door for them as they left the coffee shop. It had been a brief moment, a flicker of eye contact, but something about it felt off. Had Grim recognized them? There had been something in his eyes, a spark of curiosity or perhaps recognition. And then later, in the car park, when DarkSeraphim had blocked Grim and Clo's path, their eyes had met again. Was it just a coincidence? Or was Grim closer than they thought?

DarkSeraphim clenched the steering wheel, doubt creeping into the cracks of their confidence. *Am I losing control?* The thought made their stomach churn. They couldn't afford mistakes. Molly was too important, and failure wasn't an option.

They shook their head, forcing the doubt away. *Focus.* Molly was still theirs, still in the palm of their hand. There was no time for second-guessing now. The plan was still on track, but they needed to be more careful.

Grim was watching them. That much was clear.

But not for long.

Lisa Stewart sat alone in her sleek, modern office, the soft glow of the desk lamp casting shadows against the walls. She drummed her fingers lightly on the polished wood, her mind racing as she replayed the events of the past few days. Everything had been going so smoothly—until DarkSeraphim had fumbled the plan in Seaham.

It had been too close.

Lisa clenched her jaw, the muscles in her neck tightening with the weight of her thoughts. She had spent years carefully crafting this operation—every detail, every player had been handpicked to fit her design. She held the reins, and no one else. Certainly not DarkSeraphim, no matter how clever they thought they were.

They were useful, yes. Resourceful. But lately, their incompetence was starting to show. Letting Molly slip through their fingers in the coffee shop had nearly undone everything. Molly had recognized her at the harbour—if even the smallest seed of suspicion had been planted, it could have destroyed the entire operation. And that was unacceptable.

"You think you're in control, don't you?" Lisa thought bitterly, picturing DarkSeraphim with their smug sense of superiority. "But I know better."

Lisa was the one pulling the strings. Paul Reid, Molly's pathetic excuse for a father, was nothing more than a pawn—blackmailed and broken, dancing to her tune without even knowing who truly held the power. And Molly... Molly was the centrepiece, the key to the grander plan. Lisa had invested too much in her to let anyone ruin it now.

The more Lisa thought about it, the more her irritation grew. DarkSeraphim had been lucky so far. She had allowed them to play their part, but she was done with near misses. She needed precision, and DarkSeraphim's latest blunder was testing her patience.

"I won't tolerate another mistake," she told herself, her mind already calculating the next steps. If DarkSeraphim slipped up again, they would become a liability—one she wouldn't hesitate to remove.

Lisa's lips curled into a cold smile as she leaned back in her chair. She was still in control. The game was far from over, and no one—not DarkSeraphim, not the police, and certainly not Molly—would change that.

"They don't know who they're dealing with," she mused. "But they'll find out soon enough."

Chapter 17: Escalation and Convergence

"DI Grimshaw, this is Durham Control. checkpoints are set up near Sherburn Village, but no new sightings of the black car. Over." The radio broke the silence like a gunshot bringing both Grimshaw and Clo out of their individual darkest failings.

Clo exchanged a look with Grim. She could see the frustration etched into his face. They were close, but DarkSeraphim had been two steps ahead from the start.

"They're hiding," Clo muttered, gripping the wheel tighter. "they will have her holed up somewhere before moving her for good"

Grim nodded, deep in thought. "There aren't many places they can go. They have to be hiding out somewhere nearby. It's rural—lots of farmhouses, maybe even an abandoned building..."

He trailed off, his mind tugging at something, a thought that had been nagging at him ever since Seaham. That face in the coffee shop, the eyes in the review mirror of the car that had slowed them down in the car park. There was something familiar, something he couldn't quite place, but it gnawed at him, demanding his attention.

"I've seen them before," Grim muttered, more to himself than to Clo.

Clo shot him a curious glance. "Seen who?"

"In the coffee shop and the car," Grim said, his voice distant as the realisation began to take shape. "At the café. When I held the door for them. I recognized their eyes. And again, when they blocked us in the car park. Those eyes... I know them from somewhere."

Clo's frown deepened. "You think it's someone you've crossed paths with before? Someone you know?"

Grim's brow furrowed, frustration clear in his voice. "Maybe. But I can't place it. It's just... there's something familiar about them."

Clo nodded, though her mind was racing too. If Grim was right, if he had recognised them as someone from his past, someone he had crossed paths with before, what could it mean?

At the farmhouse, Abbie moved quietly around the kitchen, the faint clinking of plates and glasses the only sound in the otherwise still house. Molly was still unconscious upstairs, the drugs working as they always did, keeping her compliant and unaware. But as Abbie stood there, waiting for the kettle to boil, a strange feeling crept up her spine. Something wasn't right.

This wasn't what she had signed up for.

She had been with DarkSeraphim and Lisa for years now, following their orders, playing her part in the grand scheme. At first, it had seemed simple helping them, doing what needed to be done. But something about this situation felt different. Molly wasn't like the others. She was younger and more vulnerable, and there was something about her that made Abbie uneasy.

The door creaked open behind her, and Abbie turned to see Alan step inside. He moved quietly, nodding to her as he made his way to the kitchen table.

"Everything okay?" Abbie asked, though her voice was tight with the tension she hadn't yet admitted to herself.

Alan shrugged as he sat down. "DarkSeraphim wants the phone. I'm here to get it."

Abbie hesitated, glancing toward the stairs where Molly lay. "Do we really need to take it now? She's out cold. She's not going anywhere."

Alan gave her a look, his expression flat and unbothered. "No loose ends, Abbie. You know that."

Abbie nodded as she slowly removed the phone from her pocket and handed it over.

Alan paused, his hand on the door as he turned back to her. "It's what we signed up for. Don't start getting soft now."

Abbie's mouth tightened, but she didn't say anything as Alan left the room. The doubt that had been gnawing at her for days only grew stronger. She stared at the doorway for a long moment, wondering when everything had started to feel so wrong.

Upstairs, Molly stirred in the bed, her mind foggy from the sedatives. Her limbs felt heavy, too heavy to move, but somewhere in the back of her mind, alarm bells were going off. Something was wrong. The farmhouse. The food. The strange feeling of hands brushing against her skin.

She remembered... something. A shadow in the room. A soft hand had run gentle fingers over her, though she couldn't tell if it had been real or a dream. The memory was distant, blurred by the drugs, but the flicker of fear it ignited was real.

Molly tried to open her eyes, but everything felt distant like she was floating underwater. Her body refused to respond, weighed down by the sedatives coursing through her system. She was trapped in her own mind, her instincts screaming at her that she was in danger, but her body was powerless to fight back.

She tried to push herself up, but the weight of sleep pulled her back down. Even in her drugged state, Molly knew she was in danger. She just didn't have the strength to fight—yet.

As their phone buzzed on the seat beside them, DarkSeraphim glanced down. A message from Lisa: "Update, now"

DarkSeraphim gritted their teeth, frustration bubbling beneath the surface. Lisa was always pushing, always demanding more control. She acted like she was in charge, but DarkSeraphim knew better. They were the ones pulling the strings, even if Lisa thought she was the mastermind.

Moving along the track back towards the farmhouse, DarkSeraphim typed a quick response: "Molly's secure. We're moving forward."

They stepped out of the car, their mind already racing ahead to the next steps. They needed to remain calm and stick to the plan. Molly's role was coming soon, and there was no more time for mistakes. Tomorrow, Molly would be moved, along with the rest of the "delivery" Lisa had been overseeing in Seaham. There was no more time to waste.

Failure wasn't an option.

Chapter 18: The Weight of Silence

Molly's eyes fluttered open, her body heavy and weak as she lay in the unfamiliar bed. The cold, sterile air of the farmhouse wrapped around her like a suffocating blanket, making it hard to move or even think. She felt disoriented, her mind clouded with fog as she struggled to remember where she was. The events leading up to this moment swirled in her mind—vague, half-formed memories, mixing with her fear.

She had no idea how long she'd been unconscious.

As the haze began to clear, Molly's thoughts drifted back to months ago, before everything had spiralled out of control, when DarkSeraphim had entered her life. Back to a time when she still thought she could fix things with her father. It felt like a lifetime ago.

The memory was distant, but the feelings were as raw as ever.

She remembered how the house had been quiet. Molly had sat on her bed, legs crossed beneath her, staring blankly at the closed door of her bedroom. Downstairs, she could hear the low rumble of her father's voice, talking to someone over the phone, probably work-related. Paul Reid had always been busy. Always distracted by meetings, calls, or the endless demands of his career. Molly had long since given up trying to involve herself in his world. His disappointment had become a shadow that followed her everywhere silent but oppressive, weighing her down no matter what she did.

Paul had been an imposing figure in more ways than one. When he did focus on her, it wasn't with the love or support she craved, but with sharp, critical eyes. His disappointment never came with raised voices or shouting, but it was far more devastating in its quiet, subtle persistence. Each glance, each comment, was a reminder of how she wasn't enough—how she never would be enough for him.

She wasn't the daughter he wanted her to be.

Molly could still hear his voice in her head, that deep, disapproving tone that made her feel small, no matter how hard she tried to fight it. "You need to think about your future, Molly. You can't just drift through life without a plan. What are you even doing with yourself?"

His words had stung, not because they were cruel, but because they were laced with the kind of disappointment that had settled between them long ago, like a chasm too wide to bridge. Paul had never been the type to yell or lose his temper; instead, his disapproval was unspoken, but constant. Every interaction, every conversation between them, was a reminder of how she was failing to live up to the expectations he had placed on her.

Molly sighed, the ache in her chest as familiar as it was relentless. She had tried to explain it to him once—the way she felt trapped, not by her circumstances, but by the suffocating weight of his expectations. It had been like talking to a wall. Every decision she made was wrong in his eyes. Every action, no matter how well-intentioned, seemed to fall short of the invisible bar he had set for her. And no matter how hard she tried, she couldn't reach it.

He'll never understand, she had told herself over and over.

Her phone had buzzed on the bed beside her, pulling her from her thoughts. Molly had glanced at the screen, her heart skipping a beat. It had been a message from DarkSeraphim. She hadn't spoken to them since the night before, but seeing their name on the screen had brought a strange sense of comfort. They were the only person who seemed to understand her.

DarkSeraphim: "Hey, haven't heard from you. everything okay?"

Molly had stared at the message for a moment, her fingers hovering over the screen. How could she explain it all? The constant feeling of not being enough, the invisible walls that separated her from her father. Paul didn't shout or berate her, but his silence was louder than any argument could be. It loomed over her, casting a shadow she could never quite escape.

Molly: "Yeah, just another day at home. You know how it is."

The reply had come almost instantly as if DarkSeraphim had been waiting for her.

DarkSeraphim: "Your dad still on your case?"

Molly's fingers had hesitated over the keyboard. How could she put into words what it felt like to live under the weight of her father's constant scrutiny? It wasn't as though he was mean, not really. It was more that he simply didn't see her—didn't understand her. Every interaction between them felt like a test, one she was destined to fail.

Molly: "It's not like he yells or anything. He just... doesn't get me. He never has."

DarkSeraphim: "He doesn't have to. You don't owe him anything, Molly. You're your own person."

A lump had formed in Molly's throat as she read the message, her vision blurring slightly. DarkSeraphim always knew how to make her feel seen, even through the small screen of her phone. They had a way of cutting through the noise, making her feel like it was okay to be herself—no pretences, no need to be anything other than who she truly was.

She had typed back, her fingers moving faster now.

Molly: "He's always saying I need to get my life together like I don't have a plan. But I don't know... I just can't be what he wants me to be."

DarkSeraphim: "You don't need to change for him. You don't need to change for anyone. He's blind if he can't see how amazing you are. I see it, though."

A small smile had tugged at the corners of Molly's lips. DarkSeraphim had a way of pulling her out of her darkness, making her feel like she mattered. For the first time in days, the weight on her chest had lifted slightly. She wasn't alone—not really.

Her thoughts had drifted back to the last conversation she'd had with her father. It had been about her future—again. Paul's voice had been calm and measured, but each word had been like a dagger, cutting away at her sense of self.

"You need to start thinking about where you're going, Molly," Paul had said, his eyes fixed on her with that same disappointed look he always gave. "What are you doing with your time? Sitting in your room all day, talking to people online—it's not real life."

Not real life.

Molly had wanted to scream. How could he not understand? How could he not see that the people she talked to online were the only ones who didn't make her feel like she was failing at every turn? The only ones who didn't make her feel small.

"Maybe you should spend less time on that computer," Paul had said, his tone clipped. "You need real-world connections, not just... whatever that is."

Those words had echoed in her mind for days, haunting her. It wasn't that she didn't have real connections. It was that the ones she had weren't with the people in her life—they were with the people she had found online. The ones who understood her. The ones like DarkSeraphim.

DarkSeraphim: "You know I'm always here for you, right?"

The message had sat on the screen, glowing softly in the dim light of her room. Molly had read it over and over, letting the words sink in. DarkSeraphim had been there for her from the beginning, long before things had gotten this bad. Before the distance between her and her father had become a chasm too wide to bridge.

Molly: "Yeah, I know. Thanks."

But even as she had typed the words, a small voice in the back of her mind had nagged at her. Was she relying too much on DarkSeraphim? Her father didn't understand, but maybe he was right about one thing—she was spending more time with her online friends than anyone in the real world. Maybe that wasn't healthy. Maybe she was running away from the problems that were right in front of her.

She had shaken her head, pushing the thought aside. DarkSeraphim wasn't like Paul. They weren't trying to change her or control her. They wanted her to be herself, to embrace the parts of her that her father found strange or unsettling.

Her phone had buzzed again.

DarkSeraphim: "One day, you won't have to deal with any of this. You'll be free. You'll find people who really get you, who see you for who you are. I'll help you get there, You just have to trust me."

Free.

The word had lingered in her mind, tantalizing and out of reach. Freedom was what she wanted freedom from her father's expectations, from the constant feeling that she wasn't enough. But what did that even look like? How could she be free when the people around her refused to let her breathe? *She never mentions her Mother, ever.*

Maybe DarkSeraphim was right. Maybe the only way to be free was to leave it all behind.

Molly had closed her eyes, sinking back against her pillows, the weight of her thoughts pressing down on her once again. The silence in the house had been suffocating, but her phone had buzzed, a lifeline in the darkness.

DarkSeraphim was there. And for now, that was enough.

In a dimly lit room miles away, DarkSeraphim's fingers moved slowly over the keyboard, eyes locked on the screen. Molly's message had just come in, her words laced with loneliness and desperation. DarkSeraphim smiled to themselves—a small, cold smile. Molly was slipping further into their grasp, unaware of how closely she was being watched.

They typed quickly, their words calculated to soothe, to calm her frayed nerves. But every word was designed with purpose, each sentence nudging Molly closer to the edge—toward a dependence she wouldn't be able to escape.

"You just have to trust me." DarkSeraphim paused, fingers resting on the keys. It was a simple phrase, but it held so much power. Trust me. That's what Molly needed to do. She would follow wherever DarkSeraphim led, unaware of the true danger lurking behind the screen.

As the message was sent, DarkSeraphim leaned back, their eyes narrowing in the glow of the monitor. Molly was almost ready. Soon, she would be exactly where they wanted her. But they had to be patient. One wrong move, one hint of doubt, and everything could fall apart.

For now, DarkSeraphim would wait. Molly's time was coming.

Chapter 19: The Countdown Begins

DarkSeraphim pulled up outside the farmhouse, the crunch of tyres breaking the eerie stillness of the early evening. The sky overhead was heavy with clouds, casting a grey pall over the scene. DarkSeraphim stepped out of the car, their mind racing as they replayed the last few hours. Plans had changed—again. Molly needed to be moved sooner than expected, and there was no room for error.

They stood for a moment, the cold air biting at their face, and allowed themselves a single breath to steady their nerves. Inside the farmhouse, Abbie was in the kitchen, cleaning. She had a way of keeping things calm and methodical—qualities DarkSeraphim had come to rely on in moments like these. But even now, the tension was creeping in.

Without wasting time, DarkSeraphim made their way inside, shutting the door softly behind them. "We're moving Molly sooner than expected," they announced, their voice curt, purposeful. "Lisa's delivery is being arranged, and Molly has to be linked with the others before they're transported."

Abbie stilled, her hands tightening slightly around the utensils she held. "Moving her early?" she asked, her tone neutral but her unease palpable. She knew what this meant—everything was accelerating, the risks growing by the hour.

"Yes," DarkSeraphim replied sharply, their mind already on the next steps. "We can't afford any delays. A van will be here by 7:30 tonight. Make sure she's ready."

Without waiting for a response, they turned and headed upstairs, where Molly was still recovering. As they climbed the creaking steps, their thoughts raced. Molly had to be in the right state of mind for the transport. She had to remain pliable, just as the others had been. The operation was delicate, a web of control that DarkSeraphim had painstakingly built. But the threads were beginning to fray.

Molly lay still in bed, her limbs feeling heavy and sluggish as the sedatives wore off. The thick fog that clouded her mind was beginning to lift, and with it, fragments of voices from downstairs floated up to her. Her head throbbed, and her body ached, but she strained to listen, trying to make sense of what was happening.

She heard Abbie's voice, calm and measured as always, but there was another voice, one that sent a chill down her spine. It was unfamiliar—cold and detached. They were discussing something that made her stomach turn: "…moving her to join the others before sending them on."

The words rang in Molly's ears like alarm bells. Others? Sending them on? Her heart pounded as a cold realization settled in the pit of her stomach. She wasn't the only one. Whatever was happening to her was part of something larger, something far more dangerous than she had imagined. The full weight of her situation hit her like a punch to the gut. She had to get out of here—now.

Footsteps approached the door, and Molly's pulse quickened. She shut her eyes tightly, pretending to be unconscious. The door creaked open, and Molly's breath caught in her throat as she heard someone enter the room. The air shifted as the figure moved closer, hovering just above her. Her skin crawled when she felt a hand brush lightly across her cheek, then slide down her body in a way that made her stomach twist with revulsion. Every instinct screamed at her to lash out, to push them away, but a mixture of fear and determination held her paralysed.

The figure lingered for a moment longer before retreating, and Molly forced herself to remain still, listening intently until the door finally clicked shut. Only then did she let out a shaky breath, her body trembling from the tension.

They're going to move me. The thought repeated in her mind, a growing sense of panic filling her chest. She had to act before it was too late.

Downstairs, Abbie moved with practised ease, continuing to clean in the kitchen, but her mind was racing. The words DarkSeraphim had spoken rattled her. Molly was being moved earlier than planned, and the timeline had been accelerated. Everything was moving too quickly.

As DarkSeraphim made their way upstairs, Abbie's thoughts turned to her quiet rebellion. She had been complicit in too many things already, but Molly was different. There was something about her that made Abbie's conscience stir—a nagging voice that she couldn't ignore. She had to do something, however small.

Glancing around, Abbie moved quickly, slipping out the back of the farmhouse and into the yard. She crouched near the bins where she had hidden the number plates from the black car—the same ones that had been on the vehicle when Molly was taken. With quick, deliberate movements, she retrieved the plates and affixed them to DarkSeraphim's car parked in the driveway. Her hands trembled slightly as she worked, but her resolve was clear.

If the police were tracking these plates, maybe this would get their attention. It wasn't much, but it was all she could do without putting herself directly in danger. She had to believe that it would help.

Abbie returned to the kitchen just as DarkSeraphim descended the stairs. "I'll be back before the van arrives," DarkSeraphim said, heading for the door. "Make sure everything is in order."

Abbie nodded, her gaze flicking toward the clock. Six hours. Just 3 hours until Molly would be gone—moved to some unknown fate.

As Clo drove down the country lanes surrounding Sherburn Village, (the village was a small former mining village just northeast of the city of Durham surrounded by lush countryside),

The police radio in the car crackled with a call from Durham Police. "DI Grimshaw, Sergeant Harper—we've got a possible lead. A silver car matching the registration of the black vehicle you were after has been spotted in the centre of Sherburn Village, outside the post office."

Clo's eyes widened, her pulse quickening. "Silver car? Matching plates?"

"Confirmed. Same plates as the black car from the carpark, but now on a silver saloon."

Grim straightened his instincts on high alert. "Let's move. The centre of the village isn't far."

Clo spun the car around in the tight lane with the hedge scraping across the front of the car

As they sped down the road, Grim's mind raced. "If they're switching plates, this could be a way of trying to ~~through~~ *throw* them off, distract them while they slipped away"

Clo's jaw tightened, her focus razor-sharp. "This screams trafficking" they had both been thinking it. However, Clo brought the thought of it out into the open: "Usually, it's people being brought into the UK, but Molly's a local girl. What if they're moving her out?"

Grim's expression darkened, his frustration hardening into determination. "If that's the case, we're not just dealing with Molly's disappearance. There could be others—dozens, maybe more."

Fifteen minutes later, they pulled into the village, parking beside a Durham Police officer stationed discreetly across from the silver saloon. The officer greeted them with a nod. "That's the car. Same registration as the black one."

Clo glanced at Grim, her heart racing. "does that look like the same car that blocked us when we were trying to follow Molly?."

They both shared a look, coincidence?

In his study, Paul Reid sat hunched over his desk, his hands trembling as he stared down at his phone. The message to Lisa Stewart sat unsent on the screen, each word a weight pressing down on his chest. The guilt and fear had entwined themselves into an inescapable knot, and now, Paul felt like he was drowning.

His finger hovered over the send button, the weight of the confession crushing him. He had to tell someone—Lisa was the only person who knew the full extent of his mistakes. But even now, Paul wasn't sure if he could trust her. Could anyone help him? Or had he damned himself beyond redemption?

With a deep breath, Paul pressed send, the message to Lisa hurtling into the digital void.

"I need to see you, I need you"

Chapter 20: Threads Tighten

Paul sat nervously in the back corner of the café, his foot tapping anxiously under the table. His eyes flicked toward the door every few seconds, his stomach a knot of guilt, fear, and desperation. The untouched cup of coffee in front of him had gone cold, much like his hope. Molly was gone—and it was his fault. Every minute that passed deepened the pit in his chest, the weight of what he had done crushing him. He needed help—someone to take control, to fix what he had ruined. Lisa was the only person he could think of, the only one who had been there for him when everything fell apart. He had convinced himself she was his lifeline, though deep down, a gnawing doubt lingered.

The café door chimed softly as Lisa walked in, her stride confident and calculated. She moved with the grace of someone who had everything under control, her appearance immaculate as always. Paul's heart skipped a beat—relief and terror all at once. He locked eyes with her, and a warm, almost maternal smile spread across her face as she approached the table. But beneath that smile, Paul saw the cold calculation in her eyes.

Sliding into the seat opposite him, Lisa reached across the table, taking his hand in hers with a firm, reassuring grip. "Paul," she said softly, her voice smooth as silk, "you look terrible. What's going on?"

Paul swallowed hard, barely able to keep his voice steady. "I don't know what to do anymore, Lisa. I'm falling apart. Molly's gone and I… I let it happen. I'm thinking of going to the police. Maybe that's the only way to save her."

For a brief moment, Lisa's expression hardened. Her fingers tightened around his hand before her smile returned, softer now, more manipulative. She leaned in closer, her voice dropping to a whisper, as though sharing a dangerous secret. "Paul, you can't do that. Going to the police won't help. It'll only make things worse for Molly. These people… they'll hurt her if they even suspect you've gone to the authorities. You can't risk that."

Paul's breath quickened, panic rising in his chest. "But what am I supposed to do? I'd already given them all the money I had, and they still took her. I… I can't keep doing this. I'm going to lose it."

Lisa's gaze softened, her fingers brushing over the back of his hand in a gesture that was meant to calm him, but it only deepened her control. "Paul, you need to stay calm. I know this is tearing you apart, but you have to trust me. We'll figure this out together like we always have."

Paul blinked back tears, his desperation swallowing him whole. "I've ruined everything. I've ruined my family… Molly…"

Lisa's eyes glittered with something dark as she sensed his complete collapse. She tightened her hold on his hand, her voice gentle but commanding. "You haven't ruined anything, Paul. You're in a tough spot, but it's not your fault. Don't make any rash decisions. No police. And don't tell Amanda—not yet. We need to handle this carefully."

Paul stared at her, lost in a sea of guilt, uncertainty, and fear. His head swam with conflicting thoughts, but he nodded weakly, letting her words wash over him like a balm. "Okay… okay. But what do I do?"

Lisa smiled wider, her control over him absolute. "That's right. Now, I want you to go home, try to get some rest, and wait for me to call you. We'll figure out the next steps together, but trust me, Paul. We'll fix this. Just stay calm."

Paul nodded again, feeling as though the weight on his shoulders had momentarily lifted. He stood up shakily and walked out of the café, leaving Lisa alone at the table.

As soon as he was out of sight, Lisa's pleasant expression faded into a hard, calculating stare. Paul was becoming a liability. He was unravelling too quickly, and if he couldn't be controlled, she would need to find a more permanent solution. Tapping her fingers lightly against the table, her mind raced. If Paul couldn't keep it together, something drastic would have to be done.

Grim and Clo had been sitting in silence for the better part of twenty minutes, parked discreetly across from the small village post office. The silver saloon sat parked outside, its presence unnerving, as if it were just waiting for something—or someone. The same registration plates from the black car from earlier now sat on this vehicle—a clear attempt to throw them off. Clo's sharp eyes never left the saloon, while Grim's mind churned over the details, his instincts telling him they were close.

Clo broke the silence, tapping her fingers on the steering wheel. "That's definitely the car, from the car park but the plates? it is either a mistake or a miss direction, the plates were registered to the black car, we checked"

Grim leaned forward, narrowing his eyes at the saloon. "It's desperation. They're feeling the heat, and they're making mistakes. But that gives us a chance." He glanced at Clo, his voice measured. "If we're careful, they'll lead us straight to Molly."

Clo's grip on the wheel tightened. "Do we wait for someone to get in or go check it out?"

Grim kept his eyes trained on the car. His instincts were pulling him in two directions—one part of him wanted to rush the vehicle and search for clues, but the other, calmer part of him knew they couldn't risk tipping off the people involved. "We wait. Whoever gets in that car might lead us to Molly, and we can't afford to lose that opportunity."

Clo nodded, her heart racing. "So, we follow?"

Grim nodded grimly. "Exactly. If this is as big as I think it is—trafficking, not just Molly—we need to be smart. They've covered their tracks well so far, but this might be their mistake. We can't let them disappear again."

The moments ticked by in tense silence. Clo's eyes flicked to the rearview mirror, catching movement. "Grim," she said quietly, her voice tight, "someone's heading for the car."

Grim's gaze snapped forward. A woman in her thirties, dressed in a dark coat, was walking briskly toward the silver saloon. Her movements were hurried but deliberate. "Stay calm," Grim muttered, watching as the woman unlocked the door and slid into the driver's seat.

The engine came to life, and Clo's pulse quickened. "We're not losing them this time," she said, easing the car into gear, giving the saloon enough distance not to draw attention, but close enough to track.

Grim grabbed the radio. "Control, this is DI Grimshaw. The target vehicle is on the move. Requesting backup on standby."

As the saloon turned at the roundabout and out of the village, Clo followed, her hands steady on the wheel but her mind racing. "This is it. If we lose them now, Molly could be gone for good."

Grim's voice was low, filled with determination. "We won't lose them."

Back at the farmhouse, Molly's senses slowly sharpened as the sedative wore off, though her body still felt heavy and sluggish. Her skin crawled with the memory of a hand tracing her body, and she forced herself to push the horror aside. She had to stay clear-headed. She couldn't afford to panic now.

The conversation she had overheard earlier kept replaying in her mind—moving her with the others… sending them on. Whoever these people were, they weren't just after her. She was part of something bigger. Trafficking? Smuggling? Surely not, that only happened in books or movies or TV shows, not real life. Her stomach twisted with fear and disgust at the thought. Whatever it was, she knew that she couldn't stay here.

Her limbs felt like lead as she pushed herself up from the bed, her legs trembling beneath her. She bit down hard on her lip to keep from making a sound as she stood. Her body screamed in protest, but Molly forced herself to move. She had to try.

Creeping toward the window, her breath came in shallow gasps, and her hands shook. Every small noise felt like thunder in the silence. Her fingers fumbled at the latch, but just as she was about to lift it, the sound of voices floated up from outside—closer now.

Her heart pounded, a cold sweat breaking out across her skin. She froze, terrified of being caught. If they found her like this, they might drug her again—or worse.

Molly's mind raced. She had to be smart, had to bide her time. But time was running out.

Downstairs, Abbie stood in the kitchen, her hands trembling as she dried the last of the dishes. DarkSeraphim's words echoed in her head—7:30. That was when they would take Molly, when she would be sent off to God knows where, lost forever.

Abbie's heart pounded in her chest. She hadn't signed up for this. Trafficking? Moving people like they were cargo? It had all spiralled out of control, and now she was in too deep.

She glanced nervously at the clock. Two hours. There was still time—barely. The plates on the car were her only hope. If the police noticed, if they were close enough, maybe they could stop this. But what if DarkSeraphim realized what she had done? What if they found out?

DarkSeraphim's mind was spinning with thoughts of the operation. Molly's disappearance needed to be flawless. The plan was in motion—once the van arrived, Molly and the others would be moved and untraceable just like the others. They remembered the moment in Seaham when Grimshaw had held the door open for them. They knew it was him, the memory of their last encounter tugged at them like a bird pulling a worm from the ground. There had been something in his eyes—a flicker of recognition. Grimshaw wasn't like other detectives. He was dangerous and relentless. He had nearly caught them before, back when they were running part of the operation in Cornwall. They had slipped through his fingers then, and they intended to do it again now. Grim couldn't be allowed to get any closer. If he kept digging, he wouldn't just find Molly—he'd uncover the entire operation.

And that was something DarkSeraphim couldn't let happen.

Chapter 21: Darkseraphim

The silver saloon glided silently down the narrow country road, its presence unsettling in the otherwise quiet countryside. Clo kept their car at a safe distance, her eyes fixed on the vehicle ahead, her knuckles white as she gripped the wheel. The air between her and Grimshaw was heavy with tension, like the moments before a trap snapped shut. Both of them knew this could be the break they had been waiting for—or the moment when it all slipped away.

Neither of them spoke for a long while. The only sounds were the soft hum of the engine and the occasional crackle from the radio. But Grimshaw's mind wasn't quiet. His mind churned, flipping through memories like the pages of an old case file. And then, suddenly, it hit him with the force of a freight train.

"SkeletonAposal!" Grimshaw shouted, his voice cutting through the silence like a whip.

Clo jumped, her hands tightening on the wheel as the car swerved slightly before she corrected it. "What? Grim, what are you talking about?" she asked, alarm sharpening her tone.

But Grimshaw wasn't listening. His mind was racing backwards, retracing steps from two years ago—two years of frustration, dead ends, and elusive shadows. "SkeletonAposal," he repeated, this time with grim recognition. "I knew I'd seen her before. It's her. It has to be."

Clo shot him a sideways glance, her attention split between Grim and the car they were tailing. "Who? Grim, what the hell are you talking about?"

Grimshaw exhaled sharply, trying to steady the flood of memories that were crashing into him. "Two years ago, I was part of a major investigation down in Cornwall. We were chasing a trafficking ring—one of the biggest we'd ever uncovered. SkeletonAposal was the online handle for a woman who ran part of the UK operation. Her job was to seduce and manipulate minors online, luring them into the network. She was a ghost—never left a trace we could follow. And she was good. Too good."

Clo's brow furrowed, her focus darting between the road and Grim. "You think that woman—back at the café and the one we saw today—is SkeletonAposal?"

Grimshaw nodded his voice tight with conviction. "I know it's her. Those eyes... I'll never forget them. I spent over a year chasing her, watching her web stretch across the UK and into Europe. She lured kids in from all over, promising them love, safety—whatever they wanted to hear. But once they were hooked, they were gone. Some were sold into trafficking rings across Europe. Others... we never found."

A chill crept up Clo's spine. The weight of what Grimshaw was saying hit hard. This wasn't just a random kidnapping. Molly was caught in the web of someone far more dangerous than they'd imagined.

"So, what happened?" Clo asked, her voice low. "You almost caught her?"

Grimshaw's eyes darkened as he leaned back in his seat, running a hand over his stubbled chin. "It was two years ago, down in Cornwall. I'd been on SkeletonAposal's trail for months. We got close—really close—but every time, she slipped away. She knew exactly how to cover her tracks. We'd get a lead, and by the time we moved in, she'd be gone."

"There was one case," Grimshaw continued, his voice quieter now, filled with the weight of old regrets. "A girl... she was just a kid. I thought we had her. All the signs pointed to SkeletonAposal being there. We had surveillance, intel, everything in place." He clenched his jaw, his eyes staring out at the road as if he could see the moment all over again. "But we were too late. The girl was gone. SkeletonAposal had already taken her."

The memory hung in the air between them, heavy and raw. Grim rarely spoke about old cases, especially the ones that had gotten away from him. But this one clearly cut deeper than most.

"And now you think DarkSeraphim is SkeletonAposal?" Clo asked, her voice steady but laced with tension.

Grimshaw nodded again, his eyes filled with certainty. "It's her. I've been chasing this ghost for too long to be wrong about it. She's back under a new name, but the methods are the same. And Molly... she's caught up in it all."

Clo said nothing, but the realisation weighed heavily on her. The stakes had just skyrocketed. If Grimshaw was correct and DarkSeraphim was SkeletonAposal, they couldn't afford to let her slip away.

The silver saloon in front of them turned down yet another narrow country road. Suddenly, as they rounded a bend, Clo spotted something that made her stomach drop. The silver saloon was disappearing down a barely visible dirt track, its taillights catching the last rays of sunlight as it moved into the shadows of the trees.

"There!" Clo hissed, her foot easing off the accelerator as she considered her next move.

Grimshaw's heart raced. "Don't lose them."

But Clo was already thinking ahead. She drove past the turn, continuing down the road and pulling off into a small parking area hidden by trees. She switched off the engine, her breath coming in steady, deliberate gasps.

"Do you think they saw us?" she asked, turning to Grimshaw.

Grim shook his head, his eyes scanning the rearview mirror. "Not sure. But if they did, they'll know we're close."

Clo's jaw clenched as the gravity of the situation settled in. "So, what's the plan?"

Grimshaw exhaled slowly, his mind spinning through their options. "We need to get eyes on where that track leads. If it's what I think it is, then that is where they will be holding Molly."

Clo's eyes widened. "You think this is a trafficking hub? Somewhere off the grid?"

Grimshaw nodded grimly. "These networks don't operate in plain sight. They move people through hidden channels—abandoned farmhouses, warehouses, places no one would think to look. If Molly's there, she won't be alone. We need to move carefully."

Clo's determination solidified as she glanced toward the track they'd just passed. "Then let's get her out of there before it's too late."

DarkSeraphim's Calculations

In the silver saloon, DarkSeraphim's mind raced as they navigated the twisting country roads. Their eyes flicked between the rearview mirror and the winding track ahead. They knew Grim and Clo were following—they could feel it. The detective's reputation preceded him, and DarkSeraphim had always known this day might come.

The car rattled over a rough patch of road, and DarkSeraphim clenched their jaw, tightening their grip on the wheel. SkeletonAposal. The name had once been synonymous with fear and control in the darkest corners of the internet. DarkSeraphim had been her evolution—an even more elusive entity, carefully crafted to erase the vulnerabilities that had nearly brought her down before.

But Grimshaw. He was persistent—obsessed, even. He had come close to catching her two years ago in Cornwall, and she hadn't forgotten the way he had looked at her as she slipped through his fingers. That look had haunted her. And now, he was back. But this time, she wouldn't underestimate him.

The plan was already in motion. Molly was secure, hidden away with Abbie. By the time Grimshaw figured out where they were, it would be too late. Molly would be gone, moved along with the others to a safehouse far beyond Grimshaw's reach.

Almost got me. The words she had mouthed to Grimshaw from the train echoed in her mind. The memory of his furious expression brought a cold smile to her lips. This was a game she knew all too well.

But this time it felt different.

She glanced at the clock on the dashboard. The van would be at the farmhouse soon. They just needed to make sure Grimshaw was chasing shadows long enough for the transport to be completed.

Everything had to go perfectly. One wrong move, and years of careful planning and execution would unravel.

At the farmhouse, Molly's heart pounded in her chest as she crouched by the window, her breath coming in short, shallow gasps. The sedative had mostly worn off, but the heaviness in her limbs remained, making every movement slow and painful. She had heard the voices downstairs—heard the plan. She wasn't just a victim of some isolated kidnapping. She was part of something much bigger, something far more dangerous.

Her fingers trembled as she tried to pry the window open. If she could just get out, just make it to the woods, she might have a chance.

Molly's mind raced. She had to get out. She had to run.

But time was running out.

Chapter 22: Laying the Trap

Grimshaw stared down the narrow track where the silver saloon had vanished moments before, swallowed by the thick wall of trees framing its edges. The path was barely visible in the dimming light, hidden beneath a canopy of twisted branches. His gut twisted with the familiar sense of danger—it was too risky to charge in without knowing what lay at the other end. This was a delicate situation. One wrong move and Molly could disappear for good.

"We're close," Clo muttered, her fingers tapping rhythmically on the steering wheel as if trying to release the tension coiling inside her. "But we can't follow blindly. They'll know."

Grimshaw nodded, his mind racing. Clo was right. They had to be smart about this. Rushing in could spook DarkSeraphim, and if they lost her now, there might not be another chance.

Pulling out his phone, Grim quickly scrolled through his contacts until he found the number for Durham Police Control. The line clicked after two rings and a familiar voice answered.

"Durham Control, Sergeant Foster speaking."

"Sergeant Foster, this is DI Grimshaw," Grim said, his voice low but urgent. "We followed the car and it went down a track off the main road. We need to know what's down there—lay of the land, private property, any known locations that might be used for... covert operations."

Grimshaw detailed their location. There was a pause on the other end of the line, the sound of papers rustling and rapid typing in the background. Grim exchanged a glance with Clo, who was watching the road like a hawk, her foot hovering over the accelerator. They couldn't afford to lose this lead.

"DI Grimshaw," Foster's voice returned, more focused now, "the track you're describing... hold on a moment." More typing, a slight pause. "It looks like that area backs onto private land. There used to be a couple of old barns, owned by a farmer who stopped using them years ago. But recently, they were redeveloped by a private buyer. No clear records of what's happening there, but it's fenced off now—no cameras, no signs of activity that we've picked up."

Grim's pulse quickened. It was exactly the kind of place someone like DarkSeraphim would use. Secluded, inconspicuous—perfect for hiding people or moving them without being noticed. "Are those barns accessible by vehicles? Vans, trucks?"

"Affirmative," Foster replied. "The track leads to a small clearing by the barns. Plenty of space to park, load, or unload—whatever they're doing back there."

Grim cursed under his breath, his heart pounding. "This could be it. We think we're onto a major trafficking operation, possibly led by someone we've, I've been chasing for years. DarkSeraphim—have you heard that name?"

Foster's voice sharpened with recognition. "DarkSeraphim? Yeah, we've had whispers about them. No concrete evidence, but if you're saying they're involved…"

"I'm saying it's highly likely," Grim cut in. "We need eyes on that place, discreetly. Can you send backup? Unmarked vehicles, plain clothes. We can't spook them, but we can't let them get away either."

"I'll get some units moving," Foster replied, already sounding as if he was on the move. "We'll keep it quiet. You stay put until we're in position."

"Copy that." Grimshaw ended the call and turned to Clo. "Those barns have been redeveloped recently. The place is fenced off, no cameras. It's the perfect spot to hide someone like Molly."

Clo nodded her jaw tight with focus. "If we move too soon, we'll lose them. But if we wait too long, they could disappear."

Grimshaw ran a hand through his hair, the weight of the decision pressing down on him. "We're getting backup from Durham. Plain clothes, unmarked. They'll help us close in without drawing attention."

Clo glanced at him; her brow furrowed. "And if DarkSeraphim's there?"

Grimshaw's fists clenched involuntarily, his mind flashing back to Cornwall, to the train station where SkeletonAposal had slipped through his fingers. "If she's there, we bring her in. No one gets away this time."

Minutes passed that felt like hours as Grim and Clo sat in tense silence, their eyes fixed on the road ahead. Clo kept her foot hovering above the accelerator, every muscle in her body coiled and ready to react at the slightest movement. She didn't dare take her eyes off the track; the same path the saloon had vanished down earlier.

Grim's phone buzzed, breaking the silence. He glanced at the screen—it was Foster again.

"We've got two units heading toward the area now," Foster said. "ETA five minutes. They'll come in from different sides—keep it quiet, just as you requested. Are you in position?"

"We're set," Grim replied, his voice steady. "No movement from the target vehicle yet. We're parked just off the main road where the track leads. We'll follow as soon as we see an opening."

"Copy that. Hold tight until we're in position," Foster said, then paused. "Grimshaw, if this really is DarkSeraphim, you're sitting on a powder keg. Don't rush in unless you're sure."

"I know," Grim replied tightly. He ended the call and pocketed his phone. His pulse raced—this could be the moment they had been chasing for so long. Too many times, this ring had slipped through their fingers. Too many victims had vanished before they could be saved. But not this time.

Clo glanced at him; her brow furrowed with concern. "You've chased DarkSeraphim before, right? You said this was personal."

Grim exhaled slowly, his gaze fixed on the dark track ahead. "Yeah. She's always been one step ahead. In Cornwall, I came so close, but she slipped away. I thought I'd lost her for good. But now…"

"But now we've got her," Clo finished for him. "And Molly."

Grimshaw nodded, his fists clenched in his lap. "And Molly."

The weight of those words hung in the air between them. Grimshaw's mind raced as he pieced together the clues, his thoughts jumping from Cornwall to Seaham to Sherborne Village. Every lead, every scrap of evidence had brought them to this moment. DarkSeraphim was close—he could feel it.

As they waited in the tense silence, anticipation hung thick in the air. The trap was almost set. All they had to do was spring it.

Chapter 23: Moments of Decision

Molly's hands fumbled with the latch of the bedroom window, her body still sluggish. Every movement felt like wading through thick mud. Her fingers were stiff and uncooperative, her arms heavy as if they no longer belonged to her. Desperation gnawed at her insides. She could hear her mind screaming Hurry, get out, run! Before it's too late! —but her body couldn't match the urgency of her thoughts.

The latch finally began to budge, just enough to let a sliver of cold air into the room. Molly gasped, sucking in the fresh air like it was the first breath she'd taken in hours. But before she could open the window further, she heard the unmistakable sound of a door closing downstairs. Her blood ran cold. She froze, her breath catching in her throat as the faint crunch of gravel under tyres reached her ears. Someone had just left the house.

Was it Abbie? Or someone else? Her mind whirled with possibilities. This could be her chance to escape—or the beginning of something far worse. She bit her lip hard, willing herself to move faster, to break free before anyone else could return. But her fingers, still dulled by the drugs, fumbled again.

Come on. Come on! she urged herself.

The latch gave a quiet click, and Molly let out a shaky breath. She had managed to get the window open a few inches. The cold breeze slipped in, chilling her face but bringing with it a surge of hope. If she could just climb out...

Her heart pounded as she tried to lift herself onto the windowsill, her limbs trembling with effort. But just as she shifted her weight, the hair on the back of her neck stood on end. Molly froze, a feeling of dread creeping over her as though she were being watched.

Slowly, almost unwillingly, she turned around. Her stomach dropped.

Abbie stood in the doorway, arms folded across her chest, her gaze fixed on Molly. But something was different in her eyes—something that wasn't cold or threatening. Instead, it was a mix of curiosity and something else Molly couldn't quite place. Hesitation? Regret?

Molly's breath hitched, her heart hammering against her ribs. She had been caught. There was no doubt about it now—Abbie was here to stop her, to drag her back, or worse. The muscles in Molly's legs were weak, unsteady beneath her as she searched Abbie's face for a clue of what was coming next. But Abbie wasn't moving. She just stood there, watching.

For a long, agonising moment, neither of them spoke. The tension between them was almost unbearable. Molly's mind raced with a thousand questions, but one burned more fiercely than the rest. Why?

"Abbie," Molly finally whispered, her voice shaky and raw. "What's going on? Why are you doing this to me? What do you want from me?"

Abbie didn't answer right away. She stepped into the room, her presence filling the space like a heavyweight. Molly's pulse quickened. Was Abbie here to drug her again? To keep her locked away until DarkSeraphim's plans were set in motion? Every muscle in Molly's body screamed at her to run, but she couldn't move, trapped by the uncertainty of what would happen next.

The silence stretched out, the only sound was Molly's ragged breathing. Abbie's face, usually so cold and impassive, softened as her gaze dropped to the floor. For the first time since Molly had arrived at the farmhouse, she saw something flicker in Abbie's eyes—something human. Guilt. Maybe even regret.

"You need to let me go," Molly whispered, her voice breaking with emotion. "Please. I just want to go home."

Abbie flinched, her shoulders stiffening as though Molly's plea had struck her harder than she'd expected. The tension in the room shifted, something unspoken passing between them. Molly's fingers gripped the windowsill behind her for support, her heart pounding in her chest. This was it—whatever Abbie decided in this moment would change everything.

Abbie looked away, her gaze distant. The silence was deafening, stretching out for what felt like an eternity. Molly could almost hear the war raging inside her, the battle between loyalty to DarkSeraphim and the guilt that had been eating away at her.

"I can get you out," Abbie finally whispered, her voice so low it barely carried across the room. "But you need to listen to me, and you need to do exactly what I say."

Molly's breath caught in her throat, hope and disbelief swirling inside her. "You... you're going to help me?"

Abbie nodded, but her movements were slow, hesitant. Her eyes darted to the open doorway as if expecting DarkSeraphim to appear at any moment. "There's a back door that leads to the field that leads to the woods. If you follow the path straight through, you'll come to another farmhouse on the other side. They'll help you there."

Molly's heart raced. Was this really happening? Could she finally escape? But even as hope surged inside her, fear gnawed at the edges of her mind. "What about you?" she asked, her voice barely above a whisper. "What will happen to you if they find out?"

Abbie hesitated, her jaw tightening. She forced a small, strained smile that didn't reach her eyes. "I'll be fine," she said, though her voice trembled with the weight of the lie. In her heart, she knew the truth—there would be consequences. DarkSeraphim wouldn't just forgive this. They'd find out. They always did. But she couldn't think about that now. Molly needed to go. She had to be free.

"Hurry," Abbie urged, glancing at her watch, her voice more insistent now. "They'll be back any minute."

Molly nodded; her limbs shaky but fuelled by a new sense of determination. Abbie guided her toward the narrow hallway that led to the back of the house. Every creak of the floorboards sent a jolt of panic through Molly's chest, but she kept moving, her pulse hammering in her ears.

The back door creaked open, revealing the thick, shadowy woods beyond. Molly hesitated for a second, her gaze flickering back to Abbie, whose face was tight with fear and conflict.

"Thank you," Molly whispered, her voice thick with emotion.

Abbie's smile was pained, her eyes full of unspoken fear. "Go," she said firmly. "Run. Don't look back."

Molly stepped into the cold evening air, the wind rustling through the trees as she made her way toward the woods. She didn't look back.

DarkSeraphim's grip on the steering wheel was so tight that their knuckles had turned white, as she ended the call. Her pulse quickened as she strode toward the house, shoving the front door open with more force than necessary. The house was eerily quiet, but the tension in the air was palpable. Their eyes swept through the rooms until they found Abbie in the kitchen, her back turned, methodically wiping down the counters.

"Is everything ready? The van will be here in 5 minutes" DarkSeraphim's voice was sharp, laced with impatience.

Abbie barely looked up, her movements steady and controlled. "Yes," she said evenly, though her heart raced with fear. "Everything's in place."

DarkSeraphim's eyes narrowed, suspicion creeping into their mind. Something was off, but they didn't have time to dwell on it. The van would be here soon, and everything depended on getting Molly—and the others—out before Grim and Clo arrived. They couldn't afford to be sloppy now.

Satisfied for the moment, DarkSeraphim turned and headed toward the stairs to check on Molly, completely unaware that she was already gone.

[Handwritten margin note: ↑ what happened to their?]

Chapter 24: The Chase Begins

DarkSeraphim ascended the creaky wooden stairs of the farmhouse, their mind racing. The unsettling silence in the house only heightened their growing anxiety. Molly needed to be ready to move. The van would be here any minute, and everything had to be perfect—no mistakes. With each step, their pulse quickened, the rhythmic thudding of ~~her~~ boots echoing through the narrow corridor. Something felt off. A gnawing sense of unease had settled deep in their gut ever since the encounter with Grimshaw in Seaham. ~~She~~ could feel them lurking too close for comfort.

Reaching Molly's bedroom door, DarkSeraphim paused, a chill creeping down their spine. Something was wrong. The air felt colder, tighter like the house itself was holding its breath. With a forceful shove, they pushed the door open, their heart hammering in their chest.

The bed was empty.

Molly was gone.

A cold rush of panic flooded DarkSeraphim's veins as their eyes scanned the room, searching for any sign of her. They tore the sheets back as if expecting her to be hidden beneath them, but the bed was perfectly made. It was as though she had never been there at all.

Wild and frantic, their eyes darted around the room, desperate for a clue. The ensuite—she had to be in there. No way could she have escaped. Not in her sedated state. With quick, hurried steps, DarkSeraphim crossed the room and flung open the bathroom door.

Meanwhile, Molly's legs wobbled, her body heavy with the remnants of the sedative. Each step felt like pushing through thick, unyielding mud, her vision swimming slightly with the effort. Her limbs trembled, fighting every inch of movement. She had to keep going. She had to get to the woods. But her body was rebelling, weighed down by exhaustion and the drugs still lingering in her system.

Come on. Just one more step, Molly urged herself, her breath coming in short gasps as panic gripped her chest. The farmhouse was shrinking behind her, but it felt like the woods were still so agonisingly far. The cold air burned her throat, the wind whipping through the tall grass as if pushing her forward. The tree line was so close, yet her muscles screamed with every step.

She stretched her arms out for balance, her fingers twitching, like a toddler learning to walk and reaching for the safety of a parent's waiting arms, but instead, she was reaching toward the shadowy sanctuary of the woods. Almost there. Almost safe.

But the sedative was pulling at her, dragging her down, clouding her vision. The woods loomed ahead, but each step felt slower, heavier like the world itself was conspiring against her.

Just a few more feet. She could make it. She had to.

Back in Molly's room, DarkSeraphim stared at the empty ensuite, their breath catching in their throat. Molly wasn't there. She wasn't anywhere. DarkSeraphim's chest tightened, panic erupting inside them as they scanned the room again, searching for any sign of where she could've gone.

Then, out of the corner of their eye, they saw it—the window. The latch was undone, and the frame cracked open. An icy chill spread through their chest as they approached it, their heart pounding wildly. DarkSeraphim leaned out, their eyes sweeping the field behind the farmhouse, then they saw it—a small, distant figure disappearing into the edge of the woods.

Panic surged through DarkSeraphim, a sickening wave of realisation crashing over them. Molly had escaped.

"No," she whispered, their voice barely escaping their lips. DarkSeraphim gripped the window frame so hard their knuckles turned white, the breeze tugging at the curtains like the taunting smell of freedom Molly was so close to tasting.

"No!" She snarled again, their voice a low, guttural growl. Spinning away from the window, they bolted out of the room, heart thundering in their chest.

The tree line was just a few steps away now. Molly's legs felt like they were about to give out, but she forced herself forward, her breath coming in ragged gasps. The woods loomed ahead like a dark, inviting sanctuary, promising safety if she could just reach it.

Her bare feet pressed into the cold earth, each step sending a jolt of pain through her body. Her vision swam, but she focused on the dark shadows of the trees, willing herself to keep moving. She couldn't stop now. She had to make it. She had to get away.

With one final, desperate lunge, Molly reached the edge of the woods. The tall grass gave way to the underbrush as she slipped into the cover of the trees, her body collapsing against the trunk of a large oak. She pressed herself against it, her chest heaving as she struggled to catch her breath. For a moment, she allowed herself the tiniest flicker of hope.

She had made it.

DarkSeraphim burst out of Molly's bedroom, their heart racing as adrenaline surged through their veins. She was out there. She was running. And they couldn't let her get away. Not Molly. Not now.

"Abbie!" DarkSeraphim's voice was a furious roar as they flew down the stairs, boots pounding against the old wooden steps. They barely registered the sight of Abbie in the kitchen, her hands trembling slightly as she cleaned. DarkSeraphim's fury was palpable, their voice ragged and panicked.

"She's gone! Mollys escaped!"

Abbie froze, her eyes widening, but she said nothing. Guilt gnawed at her insides, but she kept her face carefully neutral, her hands gripping the edge of the counter.

DarkSeraphim didn't wait for a response. "We have to catch her. The van will be here any second"

Without another word, DarkSeraphim slammed through the back door and sprinted across the field, their eyes fixed on the distant woods—the same place they had seen Molly disappear moments before. The tall grass whipped at their legs as they ran, their chest heaving with exertion and panic. Molly couldn't be far, not in her weakened state.

But every second that passed felt like an eternity. Every footstep brought them closer to her but also closer to failure. And DarkSeraphim didn't fail!

In the quiet of their parked car, the tension inside Grim and Clo's vehicle was palpable, thickening the air as they sat just up from the track leading to the farmhouse. The quiet lane felt like a world apart from the chaos they knew was lurking at the end of it. Their eyes stayed glued to the entrance of the lane, the faint hum of the engine their only company.

The radio crackled to life, pulling them out of their tense silence. "DI Grimshaw, this is Durham Control. Backup is approaching your location."

Grim nodded, though it was Clo who responded. "Understood. We're in position." She glanced at Grim, her voice tight. "This 5 minutes has felt like a lifetime, hasn't it?"

Before Grim could respond, they both noticed movement down the lane. A plain white van trundled past their parked car, its engine grumbling quietly as it pulled into the lane leading toward the farmhouse.

Grim's gut tightened. "That's them," he muttered, his voice hardening. He exchanged a look with Clo, both knowing the stakes had just risen exponentially. The van disappeared down the narrow track, and for a moment, the world seemed to hold its breath.

"They're making their move," Clo said, her eyes narrowing as the retreating dust left by the van's tires swirled in the air. "We can't just sit here any longer."

Grim's voice was urgent. "But we've got to be smart about it."

Moments later, the sound of approaching engines signalled the arrival of their backup. Grim exhaled sharply in relief as a convoy of police vehicles pulled up behind them. The lead car, unmarked but the officers inside were clearly from Durham Constabulary, parked next to their vehicle. Grim immediately got out to meet the approaching officers, his pulse quickening with the knowledge that every second mattered.

A seasoned sergeant, her face tense and focused, approached. "DI Grimshaw?" she asked, holding out a hand.

Grim shook it firmly. "That's right. Thanks for getting here so fast."

The sergeant nodded, cutting right to the chase. "What's the situation?"

Grim quickly filled her in, explaining what they had discovered so far including the silver car parked outside the farmhouse and their strong suspicion that Molly was inside. "We've got a trafficking operation on our hands, and Molly Reid's caught in the middle of it. We think they're moving her—and possibly others—right now."

The sergeant's jaw tightened, her sharp eyes scanning the area. "We've got full support on this. If they're making their move, we need to cut them off before they get too far."

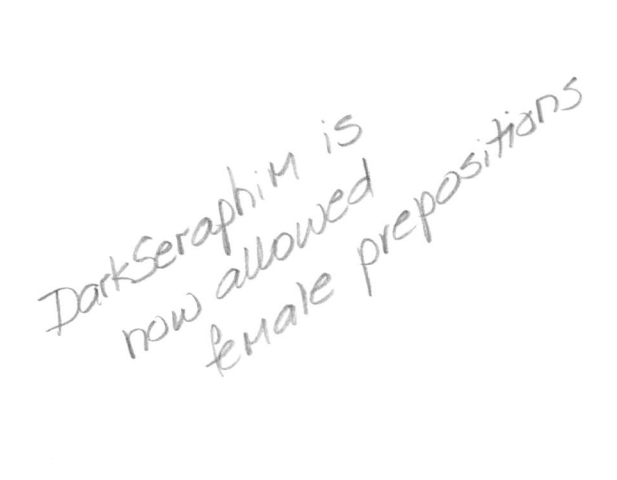

DarkSeraphim is now allowed female prepositions

Chapter 25: The Chase

Molly's breath came in ragged gasps as she fought through the thick undergrowth of the woods. Every step felt like a monumental effort. The effects of the sedative had finally worn off, but her body was still weak, her muscles trembling with fatigue. Each branch that snagged her clothes seemed like a new obstacle, every uneven step a potential downfall. But she couldn't stop—not now. Not when freedom was so close. The woods stretched out before her, vast and dark, but all she could focus on was the sound behind her.

Footsteps. Rapid, determined footsteps crashing through the trees, getting closer.

A sharp, furious voice pierced the stillness of the forest. "Molly!" The word was filled with venom and authority. DarkSeraphim. "You can't get away! There's nowhere to go!" Her voice echoed through the trees, the confidence in it sending a shiver down Molly's spine.

Her legs burned with exhaustion, her vision blurring slightly as her body fought against the weakness still clinging to her. Her foot caught on a root, and she stumbled, barely catching herself before hitting the ground. She winced in pain but forced herself back up, terror driving her forward.

Behind her, DarkSeraphim's voice grew louder, the footsteps closer. "You're going to meet your fate, Molly! One way or another!" The threat in DarkSeraphim's tone was clear, the finality a horrifying reminder of what awaited if Molly was caught.

Molly pushed her legs to move faster, her heart hammering in her chest. But every step felt like it was taking her farther away from safety. She could hear DarkSeraphim now—the rhythmic thud of boots hitting the forest floor, each one growing closer with every second.

DarkSeraphim moved through the trees with relentless precision, her breath ragged but her movements calculated. The fear of losing Molly gnawed at her, each footfall reverberating through the ground like a countdown. She could feel the pressure building inside her, the weight of Lisa's looming retribution pressing on her chest like a suffocating force. She had failed once before—failed in Cornwall—and Grim had nearly caught her.

But this time was different. This time, Molly couldn't escape. If she did, everything would come crashing down. Lisa would make sure of that.

"Molly!" she called again, her voice filled with desperation as it echoed through the dense forest. She couldn't lose Molly—not now, not after everything. DarkSeraphim's pulse quickened as she closed in on the sound of Molly's stumbling footsteps just ahead. She was so close—too close to let this slip away.

Images of Cornwall flickered through her mind—of the moment Grimshaw had almost unmasked her when she'd barely escaped with her life. That moment had haunted her every move since. She couldn't afford to fail again. Not with Molly. DarkSeraphim's mind spun with thoughts of Lisa's cold fury if she learned Molly had slipped through her grasp. Lisa's threats had always been veiled, but the consequences would be real. DarkSeraphim didn't even want to imagine what they might be.

Her breath quickened, her heart pounding in her chest as the trees blurred past her, her focus solely on the figure just within reach. Molly was close—too close to let go. She can't get away.

Chapter 26: The Nose Tightens

Grim and Clo dove back into their car, as they did Grim called through the radio "MOVE IN NOW, ALL TEAMS GO!" The cars behind them all roared into life as the offices aimed their cars at the track leading to the farmhouse, they flew along the track quicker than a greyhound chasing a rabbit. As they got to the farmhouse there was a flurry of movement in front of them, the offices shot out of the cars and the armed response unit at the front called out for everyone to remain where they were, as the two men who had just vacated the van stood paralysed with shock and fear, other armed officers converged on the open van.

Looking inside the open side door they found 10 pairs of scared eyes looking back at them as the women inside who were tied up and gagged could only look on in fear, after they gave the all clear they moved to the farmhouse itself, Grim and Clo looked at the faces in the van, all of them seemed to be of Asian decent, but they could clearly see none of them was Molly.

"She must still be inside," Grim said to Clo, their gaze turned to the farmhouse where the armed units had entered a moment earlier, they heard over the radio that they had found a female in her mid-twenties but the rest of the rooms were being cleared with no other people present in the building, Grim and Clo hurried in through the front door which leads directly into the kitchen and they saw the young woman who had been found there, "WHERE IS MOLLY!" Yelled Grimshaw "WE KNOW SHE IS HERE, TELL ME WHERE THE HELL SHE IS!"

At that moment Clo sensed a dormant beast had awoken inside of Grim, it was terrible, powerful and exhilarating all in equal measure, Abbie, tears streaming in her eyes pointed at the open back door and said she went out that way, hurry she was in terrible danger. Without a second thought Grim and Clo moved to the door and looking out across the field they could see a figure in the distance entering the woods.

Grimshaw and Clo tore across the open field, the line of woods looming just ahead. Grim's heart was pounding, his legs moving with a speed and determination he hadn't felt in months. The memory of the failed chase in Cornwall played vividly in his mind—of SkeletonAposal, the codename for the monster who had eluded him. He had been so close back then—so close to catching her, to end the nightmare she had unleashed across Europe.

But she had slipped through his fingers. And another girl had paid the price.

That thought burned inside him, fuelling the fire now raging within. He pushed harder, running faster, his eyes locked on the dark line of the woods where Molly had disappeared—and where he knew DarkSeraphim lurked. This wasn't just about Molly anymore. It was about ending a vendetta that had consumed him for years. DarkSeraphim had to be stopped. No matter the cost.

Grimshaw's breaths were ragged, but he forced the exhaustion from his mind. There was only one thing that mattered now: catching her. Stopping her. Bringing her down once and for all.

All thoughts of Molly momentarily vanished from his mind. This wasn't about saving one girl anymore—it was about redemption, about keeping the promise he had made to himself when he first took the case. DarkSeraphim had to be stopped.

Clo, running just behind him, could sense the shift in Grimshaw. She could feel the obsessive energy radiating off him—an intensity that made her stomach twist. This was no longer just another case. It had turned into something deeper for Grim—something personal, something dangerous.

"Grim!" she called out, her voice barely cutting through the pounding of their footsteps. She quickened her pace, her mind racing. She had seen this kind of drive before—in herself. And it had almost destroyed her.

For a moment, Clo's mind flickered back to her own past, to thoughts of her sister—the woman who had shattered her life, who had taken everything from her. In that moment, Clo understood exactly what Grimshaw was feeling. If this had been her chance for revenge, would she be any different? Would she be this relentless, this focused on nothing but the endgame?

The little voice in the back of her mind answered "Yes, yes She would."

But there was still Molly. There was still a girl out there, running for her life. And if Grimshaw lost sight of that, if he let his obsession consume him, they might not reach her in time.

Molly's vision blurred as she neared the edge of the woods, her breath coming in short, frantic bursts. The farmhouse Abbie had mentioned stood just ahead, its silhouette barely visible through the thinning trees. A surge of hope swelled in her chest, pushing aside the fear that had gripped her for so long. She was almost there. Almost free.

The image of freedom filled her mind, fuelling her tired legs to move faster. This nightmare was finally coming to an end. The farmhouse stood between her and her captors—her sanctuary.

But the footsteps behind her were still there. They were gaining. Her pursuer was relentless, refusing to let her slip away.

"Molly!" The voice cut through the forest like a blade—sharp, cold, calculating. DarkSeraphim. "There's nowhere you can go, nowhere to hide where I can't find you!" Her voice dripped with venom, but Molly could hear the desperation beneath it, clawing its way to the surface. DarkSeraphim was getting closer.

"You don't belong anywhere! You'll never be understood! You've never had a home, and you never will!"

The words twisted in Molly's mind, threatening to pull her back into the depths of hopelessness. But she shook her head, fighting the voice, fighting the fear. She wasn't going to let it win—not now. Not when she was so close.

With a final burst of energy, Molly stumbled out of the woods, her feet hitting the uneven surface of the farmyard. Her vision tunnelled, her focus narrowing to a single point: the farmhouse. She didn't notice the derelict state of the yard—the overgrown grass, the broken-down barn to the side. She didn't see the sagging roof or the cracked, dirty windows. All she saw was the slightly open door—a gateway to what she believed was safety.

Without thinking, Molly sprinted across the yard, her heart pounding louder with each step. She reached the door, threw herself inside, and slammed it shut, leaning against the weathered wood. Her chest heaved as she struggled to catch her breath, her eyes darting around the room in a frantic search for hope.

For a brief moment, she allowed herself to believe she was safe.

DarkSeraphim pushed harder, her breath harsh and uneven as she burst out of the woods. Her eyes instantly locked on the farmhouse door, just as it slammed shut. Her heart sank, a hollow feeling opening up in her chest.

"No..." she whispered, her worst fear creeping up her spine. Not again. Not after everything. Molly was going to slip through her fingers. Again.

For a moment, panic seized her. This couldn't happen. Not this time. Lisa would never forgive her if Molly got away.

But then, DarkSeraphim's eyes flicked around the yard, taking in the dilapidated barn and the broken windows of the farmhouse. Her fear began to subside, replaced by cold, calculating certainty. There was no one here. The farmhouse was abandoned—had been for years by the look of it. Molly was alone. No one was coming to help her.

A slow smile spread across DarkSeraphim's face, her pace slowing as she crossed the yard. She called out again, her voice dripping with false sympathy. "You're trapped, Molly! There's no one here to help you! You're all alone, just like you've always been. No one's coming to save you. You'll never escape who you are. You'll never belong anywhere."

Her voice echoed in the empty yard, bouncing off the walls of the farmhouse. DarkSeraphim knew she had Molly now. There was nowhere left for her to run.

Molly quickly and quietly made her way up the ~~straits~~ stairs knowing she had to find somewhere to hide, the fear growing inside her as she heard the calls from the yard outside, she scanned each room as she went looking for somewhere that she could use and hope to disappear into. Each room was empty and run down, it reminded her of a horror movie that she had watched with Sarah and felt a pang of pain and regret that she hadn't been able to talk to her best friend about how she was feeling.

The thought of her best friend made her realise just how much she had lost. She wanted to see her and her mam and even her dad, she felt like a small child who was scared of the dark, she thought more of her dad, their relationship had broken up so much from how it used to be but even now she knew or maybe hoped he would want to protect her, if only she knew he was the reason she was in the situation she was in, in more ways then one. → does she know? Very unclear how?

She got to the final room and saw a large old wardrobe, she moved to it as she heard the kitchen door close downstairs. She wanted to hide in it but as she moved the door it made a small squeak, worried this might give away where she was, she ducked behind it and thought again of her family and how she would never see them or her friends again. As this thought ran through her mind a tear leaked out of her eye and drained down her cheek and dropped soundlessly on to the dust covered floor.

Chapter 27: The Confession

Paul stepped into the house, his mind still buzzing from his meeting with Lisa. The conversation they'd had replayed in his mind, each word cutting into him, sharp and unforgiving. His stomach churned, an uneasy mix of guilt and relief battling for dominance. He'd been dreading this moment for weeks, knowing that Amanda would sense something was terribly wrong. After months of living with the weight of his lies, the truth was now a monster clawing its way to the surface.

The door clicked shut behind him, the sound barely registering over the pounding of his own heart. He was bracing himself, preparing for the inevitable confrontation when he heard her footsteps—quick, angry, echoing down the hallway. Amanda was coming, and Paul knew immediately that she had found out. Somehow, she knew everything.

He glanced up just as Amanda appeared, her face hard and her eyes blazing with a fierce, accusatory glare. There was no hiding now.

Paul's heart sank like a stone. She knew. She knew it all. The affair, the blackmail, the deceit—it was written across her face in anger and pain. For a moment, Paul felt the familiar urge to retreat, to deny, to hide. But there was no hiding from this. The moment had come, and the weight of it was unbearable.

Amanda came to a halt in front of him, her arms crossed over her chest, her posture tense and unyielding. Paul's pulse quickened. He had been expecting this moment, dreading it, rehearsing a thousand apologies in his head. But none of them felt sufficient. What could he possibly say?

Before Paul could speak, Amanda broke the silence, her voice trembling with barely contained emotion. "I just got a call from the police station," she said, her tone sharp and clipped. "They have a lead on Molly."

For a moment, Paul's mind went blank. The words didn't register right away, lost in the swirl of guilt and fear that had consumed him. He had been preparing for a different kind of conversation, one about his affair with Lisa, about the lies he had been feeding Amanda for months. But Molly? A lead on Molly?

The tightness in Paul's chest loosened slightly, replaced by a strange, almost disorienting sense of relief. Could it be true? Could Molly be found?

"They couldn't give me more details," Amanda continued, her voice cracking, "but it's credible. They said they think they're close."

Paul stared at her, the surge of hope rising within him momentarily overwhelming the crushing guilt. Molly—his daughter, his sweet Molly—might be alive. Might be found. For the briefest of moments, Paul allowed himself to imagine it. Molly coming home, safe, free from the nightmare she had been dragged into, that he had forced her into.

But then the reality of his situation came crashing down. The weight of everything he had done—the lies, the affair, the blackmail, the part he had played in Molly's disappearance—pressed down on him like a vice. He couldn't keep it from Amanda any longer. He couldn't live with this secret. The guilt was suffocating, and the truth was clawing its way out.

Amanda, ever perceptive, noticed the strained look on his face, the tension that had nothing to do with Molly. Her brows furrowed, her voice softening as concern bled into her features. "Paul, what's going on?" she asked, her voice trembling. "There's something else, isn't there?"

His throat felt tight, constricting with the words he needed to say but couldn't find the courage to speak. The truth was too ugly, too tangled. But there was no way out now. His voice cracked when he finally spoke.

"I need to go to the police station," Paul muttered, barely able to meet her eyes. "You... you need to drive me there. I... I can't do this alone."

Amanda's eyes widened, confusion and dread mixing on her face. "What are you talking about, Paul? What do you need to report?"

Paul shook his head, unable to look at her. "I can't explain now," he whispered, his voice hollow. "I just need to get to the station. Please. Just take me there."

Amanda was silent for a long moment, her mind racing with a thousand questions. But when she saw the desperation in Paul's eyes, the utter defeat etched into his features, she reluctantly nodded. Without another word, they grabbed their jackets and headed out the door.

The car ride was suffocating in its silence. Amanda's knuckles were white as she gripped the steering wheel, her eyes flicking toward Paul every few minutes, her mind reeling. She had seen Paul like this before, months ago, when his dad had passed away and he started spending more time in the office. He was haunted then, just as he was now, but this felt different—heavier. There was something else he was hiding, something that terrified her to think about.

She broke the silence, her voice tight with tension. "Paul, what is so important that you need to go to the police now? Is this about Molly? Is it about the lead?"

Paul didn't respond right away. He stared out the window, watching the familiar streets pass by his heart heavy with shame and fear. His breath fogged up the glass as he fought the urge to cry, to scream, to let it all out. But all he could manage was a quiet, broken, "It's my fault. All of it."

Amanda's grip tightened on the wheel, her jaw clenching. The weight of his words settled over her like the shadow of a reaper. She wanted to scream, to demand that he explain himself, but something in Paul's voice—something in the way he looked so utterly defeated—stopped her.

They pulled into the small parking lot outside the Houghton-le-Spring police station, located just up the road from Molly's school. The station looked so unassuming, so ordinary, but it loomed large in Paul's mind as the place where everything would come to light. Where his life, his lies, would be stripped bare.

Amanda parked the car and turned to him, her voice trembling with fear and frustration. "Paul, what is your fault? What are you talking about?"

Paul took a deep breath, his hand shaking as he reached for the door handle. He couldn't bear to look at her, couldn't stand the thought of the pain he was about to cause. "I love you, Amanda," he whispered, his voice thick with emotion. "But I have to do this. I have to tell them."

Before Amanda could respond, Paul opened the door and stepped out of the car. He stood for a moment, staring at the small, unassuming police station. This was it. The moment he had been dreading, the moment he had been running from. With a deep breath, he walked inside, his footsteps echoing in the quiet reception area.

The duty sergeant behind the desk glanced up as Paul approached, his expression neutral but attentive. "Can I help you, sir?"

Paul swallowed, his throat dry. "I need to speak to someone. I need to report a crime. My crime."

The sergeant's eyes narrowed slightly in confusion. "Your crime?"

Paul nodded, his voice cracking. "Everything that's happened... it's all my fault. I need to confess."

The sergeant hesitated for a moment, then motioned toward the doors leading to the back. "Come with me."

Paul followed the sergeant into a small interview room, the walls bare except for a camera mounted in the corner. The sergeant gestured for him to sit and then stepped out, leaving Paul alone with his thoughts. The weight of what he was about to do pressed down on him like a suffocating blanket. He could feel the walls closing in, the air thick with the gravity of his decision.

Outside, in the reception area, Amanda paced nervously, her mind racing. She hadn't seen Paul this distraught. The fear gnawed at her, making her stomach twist. When the sergeant reappeared, Amanda rushed over, her voice trembling. "My husband—Paul Reid. He came in here. Where is he?"

The sergeant gave her a sympathetic look. "He's being interviewed. He said he came in to confess to a crime."

Amanda's face went pale, her knees buckling slightly. The sergeant moved quickly, catching her arm and helping her to sit down. "Take a moment, ma'am," he said gently, guiding her to a chair. "I'll get you some water."

Amanda sat, her mind spinning. Paul was confessing to something. But what? What had he done?

Inside the interview room, Paul sat hunched over the table, his hands trembling as he stared at the bare walls. The silence was oppressive, the weight of his guilt pressing down on him like a crushing avalanche. He rubbed his sweaty palms against his thighs, trying to calm himself, but the effort was futile. His mind was racing, filled with images of Molly, of Lisa, of the web of lies he had spun and now couldn't escape.

The door opened with a soft click, and two detectives entered the room, their expressions calm but focused. Paul could sense the shift in the air—they knew something big was coming.

Detective Inspector Hawthorne, a woman in her early forties with short dark hair and sharp eyes, placed a small digital recorder on the table between them. Beside her was Detective Sergeant Miller, a younger man with a serious expression and a notepad in hand. They exchanged a brief glance before DI Hawthorne pressed the record button.

"The time is 7:35 PM," she began, her voice steady. "This is Detective Inspector Hawthorne and Detective Sergeant Miller interviewing Paul Edward Reid regarding a voluntary confession. For the benefit of the tape, Mr. Reid, can you please state your full name?"

Paul swallowed hard, his throat dry before answering, "Paul Edward Reid."

Chapter 28: Confessions and Revelations

Junior Detective Samantha Crews sat at her desk in the bustling incident room at Washington Police Station, the familiar hum of urgent voices and ringing phones swirling around her. The Molly Reid case had dominated the station's atmosphere for the day or so, and the pressure was clear in the strained faces of every officer. Samantha had been meticulously combing through the latest updates, but nothing concrete had surfaced in the last few hours. Time was slipping away, and so was their hope of finding Molly alive.

Suddenly, the shrill ring of her phone broke through her concentration. She snatched it up, her voice sharp and alert. "Crews."

"Samantha, it's Sergeant Johnson from Houghton Station," came the urgent voice on the other end. "Paul Reid has come in. He's confessing to a crime—something about his daughter Molly."

Samantha froze, her heart skipping a beat. Paul Reid? Confessing to a crime? Her pulse quickened as she absorbed the news. What the hell is going on? Paul Reid had been a concerned father, devastated over his daughter's disappearance. What could he possibly be confessing to?

"What kind of confession?" she asked, her voice wavering despite her attempt to remain calm.

"Not sure yet," Johnson replied, his tone brisk. "He's already in one of the interview rooms with detectives."

Samantha's mind raced. Grimshaw and Clo had to be informed immediately. She grabbed her phone and quickly dialled Grim's number, but it rang several times with no answer. Where were they? She cursed under her breath, trying Clo's number next, but got the same result—nothing.

Frustration and worry mounting, Samantha slammed the phone down onto her desk. She bolted from the incident room and rushed down the hall toward Chief Inspector Adams's office, not bothering to knock as she burst in. Adams, already deep in conversation with another officer, looked up in surprise.

"Sir, I just got a call from Houghton Station. Paul Reid has come in to confess—something about Molly. I tried calling Grim and Clo, but neither of them are answering. I need to get there now," she said breathlessly.

Adams's expression hardened as he processed the information. "Paul Reid is confessing?" he repeated in disbelief. "Get to Houghton Station fast. I'll try to reach the Durham team leading the raid. They might be able to contact Grimshaw and Clo."

Samantha nodded and bolted from the office, her heart pounding as she navigated the narrow corridors of the station. She hurried past her colleagues, barely noticing their curious glances, and rushed out to her car. The drive to Houghton-le-Spring was a blur, the buildings and streets flashing by as her mind raced with the implications of Paul's confession. What had he done? What was he hiding?

When Samantha arrived at the small Houghton-le-Spring Station, she immediately noticed a lone figure pacing near the entrance—Amanda Reid. Even from a distance, it was clear that Amanda was deeply distressed, her movements jittery and her face pale. Samantha's heart sank further. Whatever Paul was confessing to, Amanda had no idea. The weight of the situation hit her harder as she realised how little Amanda knew—and how much Paul had been hiding.

Without pausing to speak to Amanda, Samantha hurried inside. The desk sergeant, Johnson, was already waiting for her and quickly ushered her toward the back. "Paul Reid's in interview room two. Detectives Hawthorne and Miller are with him now," he said, his voice tight with urgency.

Samantha followed closely behind, her heart pounding as they approached the viewing room. She caught a glimpse of Amanda as she passed, her hands shaking uncontrollably as she lingered near the reception area. Samantha bit her lip, wondering whether Amanda had begun to suspect the truth—that Paul's confession could shatter their lives forever.

Johnson led her to the observation room, where she could watch the interview without interrupting. Through the one-way glass, Samantha saw Paul Reid slumped in a chair, his face gaunt, his eyes hollow with guilt and exhaustion. His hands trembled as they lay clasped together on the table. She pressed her hand against the glass, leaning forward as Paul's words reached her ears.

"I didn't know how to stop it," Paul said, his voice hoarse and thick with regret. "I... I was weak. I made one mistake, then another to cover it up... and then it just spiralled out of control. Everything kept getting worse."

Paul's eyes were swollen and red-rimmed from hours of crying, the weight of his confession crushing him. His hands shook as they rested on the table, and Samantha could see the sheer magnitude of the guilt he carried. Her stomach tightened as she braced herself for the full revelation.

"It started months ago," Paul continued, barely managing to keep his voice steady. "I had an affair. It was with a woman from work named Lisa Stewart. I thought it didn't mean anything... I thought I could just forget about it. But then I started getting messages. Threats."

DI Hawthorne and DS Miller exchanged a glance but remained silent, letting Paul speak. Samantha, from her vantage point, leaned in closer, her heart pounding with the implications.

"I didn't know what to do," Paul admitted, his voice cracking. "The messages... they said they knew about the affair, about everything. And they wanted money. I thought if I just paid them, it would stop. But it didn't. The demands kept coming... and then Molly..." His voice broke, tears filling his eyes. "They took Molly."

Samantha's blood ran cold. They took Molly. Paul had been blackmailed—extorted. And now his daughter was gone because of it. The full weight of his confession began to sink in. He had been entangled in something far bigger than an affair, and Molly had paid the price.

In the interview room, Paul continued, his voice growing weaker as the guilt consumed him. "I should've gone to the police. But I was scared—terrified that everything would come out. I thought I could fix it. I thought I could protect her. But I failed her. I failed my daughter."

Hawthorne's voice was calm but probing. "Mr. Reid, who sent the messages? Did you ever meet the person behind the threats?"

Paul shook his head miserably. "No... I never met them. The messages came from someone calling themselves DarkSeraphim. That's all I know."

Samantha's heart stopped. DarkSeraphim. The name that had reached out to Molly and offered her safety and freedom. The elusive online figure they now beloved to be linked to multiple trafficking operations. Paul had been blackmailed by the very person Molly thought was her saviour.

Meanwhile, outside in the waiting area, Amanda Reid sat motionless, her hands clenched tightly together in her lap. Her face was pale, her eyes wide with fear and confusion. She had no idea what Paul was confessing to, but she could feel the storm building. The uncertainty gnawed at her, each passing moment adding to the weight of dread pressing on her chest.

What had Paul done?

She glanced toward the reception desk, wondering if she should demand answers—if she should storm into the interview room and confront him—but something kept her frozen in place. What could he be confessing that he hadn't told her? Her mind raced with terrifying possibilities, each worse than the last.

Back in the interview room, Paul's voice cracked as he continued his confession. "I didn't know who DarkSeraphim was. I still don't. But they took Molly because of me. Because of my mistakes."

Hawthorne's face remained impassive, but her eyes were sharp with understanding. "You're saying the person who blackmailed you—DarkSeraphim—abducted Molly?"

Paul nodded, fresh tears sliding down his face. "Yes. And I was too much of a coward to tell anyone."

Samantha's mind raced. DarkSeraphim had Molly, and Paul's affair had been the trigger. He had been blackmailed for months, trying to handle it on his own, thinking he could outmanoeuvre the threats. But now, Molly was gone, and Paul was breaking under the weight of his guilt.

DI Hawthorne leaned forward; her voice steady but pressing. "Mr. Reid, you said Lisa arranged everything for the affair. Do you think... could Lisa have been working with DarkSeraphim?"

Paul's head snapped up, his face going pale at the suggestion. "What? No! Lisa would never—she loved Molly!"

Hawthorne pressed on, undeterred. "Think about it, Paul. DarkSeraphim knew everything about the affair—your movements, your secrets. Could Lisa have been part of this?"

Paul's mind spun, unable to reconcile the suggestion. Lisa, the woman he had trusted, the woman he had been entangled with, had been so careful. But the doubt gnawed at him now. How had they been found out? Could Lisa have betrayed him? Had she been working with DarkSeraphim all along?

"I don't know," Paul whispered, his voice barely audible. "I don't know if she was involved. But it doesn't make sense."

Hawthorne's voice was firm but compassionate. "Paul, sometimes the people we trust the most can betray us in the worst ways, I'm sure your wife would agree! If Lisa was part of this, you need to tell us. It could be the key to finding Molly."

The weight of her words hung in the air as Paul buried his face in his hands, the full magnitude of his choices crashing down on him. His love for Lisa, his betrayal of Amanda, his failures as a father—it was all tied up in this web of deceit. And now, Molly was suffering because of him.

Chapter 29: The Final Approach

Grimshaw and Clo exploded out of the woods and into the farmyard, adrenaline coursing through their veins. The transition from the dense forest to the derelict farm was jarring, and for a moment, everything stood still. The once-functional barn, now empty and worn, stood as a shell of its former self. The windows of the farmhouse were dark and cracked with years of neglect. Despite its desolate appearance, both knew Molly had run here, seeking refuge.

Clo's sharp eyes flickered toward the farmhouse, instantly noticing movement. "Look," she whispered, gripping Grimshaw's arm. They both froze, catching sight of a shadow moving past the downstairs kitchen window—quick, elusive.

Grimshaw's pulse quickened. Could this be it? Could this be the moment I finally put an end to this? Years of chasing shadows and missing girls flashed through his mind—faces he had failed to save. Especially the one in Cornwall, the girl who had slipped through his fingers. He had lived with that failure for too long. Today, there would be no more slipping away.

Grimshaw's grip on his gun tightened as he removed it from its holster, they crept closer to the house, their movements careful. Every footstep felt measured and deliberate, the gravity of the moment hanging between them. The farmhouse door hung slightly ajar, and Grimshaw shot Clo a look—they were in. DarkSeraphim was inside. They had to be.

Upstairs, Molly crouched in the far corner of the final bedroom, tucked behind the old wardrobe. Her breath came in sharp, ragged bursts, her chest tight with panic. It felt like the walls were closing in around her, the darkness pressing down, making it impossible to breathe. Panic bubbled up inside her like a rising tide, threatening to choke her. You have to calm down, she told herself. If you lose it now, you'll never make it out and never see them again.

Molly pressed her palms to the floor, grounding herself, trying to find something solid amidst the chaos of her mind. Her heart was racing, but her thoughts became clearer. No more running. No more hiding. She had no choice but to fight if it came to that. There was nowhere else to go. She couldn't keep fleeing forever.

The memory of DarkSeraphim's voice echoed in her mind, chilling her to the bone. The sickly-sweet way DarkSeraphim had spoken to her, the false promises, the manipulation, she could see it now, it had been a trap, and now it was haunting her. How long before she found her? Before those cold hands reached out to drag her back into the nightmare.

Downstairs, DarkSeraphim moved silently past the same kitchen window where Grimshaw and Clo had just seen the shadow. She was too absorbed in her hunt to notice the detectives creeping closer. Her mind was singularly focused on one thing—finding Molly. Her breath came in hard, jagged gasps—not from exhaustion but from the mixture of the thrill of the hunt and the rising panic of failure. Not again. Molly can't get away.

DarkSeraphim's footsteps were barely audible on the worn wooden floors as she swept through the downstairs rooms, methodically checking every space. The silence of the farmhouse was almost suffocating. Each door she opened, each empty room, only increased her agitation. Molly couldn't have gotten far. The thought gnawed at her, fuelling her desperation.

With a sharp intake of breath, DarkSeraphim began climbing the stairs. "Molly..." she called, her voice dripping with mock care, echoing through the hollow farmhouse. "Come out, darling. There's nowhere left to go."

Her voice carried through the darkened rooms, laced with sinister undertones. "You know no one understands you, Molly. They never did, did they? You've always been alone. No one can help you as I can."

Her words were calculated, every syllable a twisted attempt to lure Molly out. This was the game she had played so many times before preying on the vulnerabilities of her targets, isolating them and making them believe there was no other way. DarkSeraphim revelled in control, but now, as she moved closer to Molly, she felt it slipping from her grasp.

Outside, Grimshaw and Clo approached the kitchen door, the unmistakable sound of a female voice filtering through the silence. Her taunting words sent a chill down Grimshaw's spine. Molly's still alive, he thought, and the voice, it has to be DarkSeraphim, the realisation flooding him with renewed energy. DarkSeraphim's cruel taunts confirmed it—Molly was hiding somewhere in the house, but she was still alive.

Clo glanced at Grimshaw, her voice barely a whisper. "Should we call for backup?"

Grimshaw shook his head firmly, his eyes dark with determination. "We don't have time. If DarkSeraphim knows we're here, Molly's life could be in even more danger. We go in now—by the book."

Clo nodded, her heart pounding as they slipped inside the farmhouse. The house was eerily quiet, save for DarkSeraphim's distant voice echoing from upstairs. Grimshaw and Clo moved with silent precision, their training kicking in as they cleared each room on the ground floor.

Every step they took was with practiced precision, ensuring that no corner went unchecked. The tension was suffocating, each second feeling heavier as they worked their way through the darkened rooms. The kitchen was abandoned, save for a few scattered footprints in the dust on the floor. The sitting room was empty, save for some broken old furniture that was covered in layers of dust.

Grimshaw's mind raced. His instincts were screaming—they were getting closer. Every creak, every sound from above made his heart beat faster. They reached the hallway, and Grimshaw gestured toward the staircase. Up there. Clo's eyes followed his gaze, her breath catching as they both heard the unmistakable sound of creaking floorboards directly above them.

DarkSeraphim was upstairs and so was Molly.

Upstairs, DarkSeraphim stood just outside the final bedroom door, her hand resting lightly on the old, worn handle. A sinister smile curled her lips as she continued her taunts. "You never fit in, Molly. No one ever really cared about you. But I do."

Her voice softened, almost becoming a whisper. "I'm the only one who understands you, Molly. You can't run from me."

The door creaked as DarkSeraphim pushed it open, her eyes scanning the darkened room, her pulse quickening. Somewhere in this house, Molly was trembling, hiding like the frightened girl she was, and DarkSeraphim knew that fear all too well. It gave her power—control.

But before she could step further into the room, the faintest sound from downstairs caught her attention. A door closing? The noise was almost imperceptible, but it sent a jolt of panic through her. No... it can't be.

She turned sharply, retreating from the doorway. Someone else was here.

DarkSeraphim stood frozen at the top of the stairs, her heart hammering against her ribcage. The creak of the door closing downstairs echoed through her mind like the toll of a bell. Was it him? Could it be Grim?

Her breathing grew shallow, panic gnawing at the edges of her composure. She had spent years avoiding him, outwitting him, staying one step ahead. But this time felt different. This time, she was cornered.

Her mind raced. If Grim had found her, if he was here, then everything was about to fall apart. The realisation hit her like a sledgehammer. Molly was still within her grasp, but that grip was loosening with every second Grimshaw was inside this farmhouse. If Grim's here, they've already found the van, and the entire operation is unravelling.

Two paths lay before her. She could cut her losses and run, disappear into the shadows like she had so many times before. But fleeing this time didn't just mean escaping Grim—it meant facing Lisa and Lisa wouldn't tolerate another failure. The consequences of letting Molly slip through her fingers would be worse than any prison sentence. Lisa's wrath was a fate she feared even more than being caught.

Her other option was to continue the hunt. Molly was still somewhere inside this house, hiding like a cornered animal. If DarkSeraphim found her, she could still complete the job. She could still hand Molly over to Lisa and salvage the operation—and Lisa's forgiveness. But Grim was closing in, and she could feel the weight of his presence bearing down on her like a predator stalking its prey. Was it worth the risk?

Her thoughts spiralled between fear and pride. Could she outsmart Grimshaw again? Or was this the end of the line?

In the bedroom, Molly crouched lower, her knees pulled up to her chest. Her heart pounded erratically, the adrenaline and fear clouding her thoughts. She tried to stay as still as possible, listening to the faint sounds coming from outside the room and downstairs, but it was hard to focus. Her mind kept drifting back—to her parents, to the choices she had made that had led her here.

If I hadn't run away... if I'd just talked to them, would I still be safe right now?

The continued thought of her mother and father filled her with deep, aching regret. She had always felt misunderstood and out of place, but now she wished more than anything to be back home—safe, away from the terror that gripped her now.

She had been so sure that running was the only answer. That getting away was the only way to make sense of the confusion and pain that had torn at her. But now, she wished more than anything that she had never left. I didn't mean for any of this to happen...

Another tear slipped down her cheek, but she quickly brushed it away, forcing herself to stay silent. There was no time for tears now. DarkSeraphim was hunting her, and the fear of being found outweighed everything else. I have to stay strong. I have to survive this.

She took a deep breath, trying to calm her racing heart, her body still trembling from the residual effects of the sedative. Mom, Dad... I'm so sorry. I love you.

DarkSeraphim entered the room, spotting the wardrobe door slightly ajar and she smiled, "I have you now" she thought, as she opened the door she found it was empty, then she heard the faintest breath from behind the wardrobe and she moved round the side.

Chapter 30: The Battle for Survival

The moment exploded into chaos.

DarkSeraphim had expected to find Molly trembling, cowering like the frightened prey she had always imagined her to be. Her hand gripped the edge of the wardrobe, heart pounding as she prepared to pounce on the helpless girl she had spent so long manipulating. But what DarkSeraphim wasn't prepared for was the sudden explosion of fury that met her.

With a wild, primal scream, Molly launched herself at DarkSeraphim, her fingers curled like claws, reaching for her face. The scream tore through the air, filled with raw emotion—fear, anger, desperation—all melded into one violent outburst. Molly's rage consumed her, and in that moment, she forgot everything else. She forgot she was just a fourteen-year-old girl. She forgot that DarkSeraphim was a fully grown woman, far stronger than her. All she could think about was survival. All she could feel was the boiling fury that had been festering inside her throughout her captivity.

The lies. The betrayal. The manipulation.

The anger that had been simmering inside her finally erupted in a desperate attempt to regain control over her own fate.

DarkSeraphim staggered, caught completely off guard by the intensity of Molly's attack. Molly's fingers raked at her eyes, her scream ringing in her ears. DarkSeraphim instinctively raised her hands to defend herself, but she was too slow. She stumbled backward, the bed catching her off balance, and as she fell onto the old mattress, the sharp pain of the broken springs dug into her back, making her gasp in pain. Molly didn't relent. She kept clawing, her nails scratching at DarkSeraphim's face and arms, driven by fury and the primal need to fight back.

Molly's screams filled the room, an unrelenting expression of her anger, drowning out everything else. Her mind was a whirlwind of rage. She was no longer scared. This wasn't about fear anymore—this was about revenge. She wanted to punish DarkSeraphim, to make her feel every ounce of pain, confusion, and betrayal Molly had experienced during her captivity.

Down the hall, Grim and Clo were nearing the final room when Molly's piercing scream ripped through the air. They froze, exchanging a tense glance, their hearts racing. The scream was loud, filled with raw emotion—but it wasn't fear. It was something else. It sounded like anger.

They sprang into action, rushing down the hall toward the source of the sound, their weapons still drawn. Grim's mind raced. Molly was in danger—he could feel it. He didn't know whether it was her or DarkSeraphim screaming, but the urgency of the moment fuelled him forward. He burst into the room, his gun raised, shouting, "Police! Stay where you are!"

But Molly's screams drowned out his voice. Her wild, primal fury dominated the room. Grim's eyes swept over the scene in an instant. Molly was on top of DarkSeraphim, the two bodies struggling violently on the bed. Molly's hands were clawing at DarkSeraphim's face, her young face contorted with a rage so intense that it shocked Grim. This wasn't the terrified girl he had expected to find. This was someone completely different—a girl who had been pushed beyond the edge of fear and into a full-blown fight for survival.

"Molly!" Grim shouted, trying to cut through the chaos.

Clo entered the room just behind him, her eyes taking in the scene. She holstered her weapon immediately. Grim did the same and moved toward the bed, his heart pounding in his chest. "Molly," he muttered, she was fighting with everything she had and it wasn't just survival fuelling her—it was the need to punish. To release every ounce of fury she had stored inside her during her captivity.

Grim lunged forward, grabbing Molly around the middle, trying to pull her off DarkSeraphim. But Molly, fuelled by adrenaline and rage, barely registered his presence. All she knew was that someone was trying to stop her from punishing DarkSeraphim—and she wasn't ready to stop.

"Let me go!" Molly screamed, thrashing wildly against Grim's grip. "I won't let her get away! She lied to me! She ruined my life!" Her voice was raw, filled with all the emotion she had been holding back for so long.

Grim struggled to hold onto her, his hands gripping her tightly but as gently as he could, trying to restrain her without hurting her. "Molly, stop!" he shouted over her screams. "I'm here to help! I'm here to bring you home—to your parents! You're safe now!"

Molly's wild thrashing slowed for a moment, his words cutting through the fog of fury and adrenaline that clouded her mind. Her breath came in sharp, ragged gasps, her body still shaking with the need to fight. "Home?" she whispered, her voice barely audible. "My parents?"

"Yes," Grim said, his voice firm but reassuring. "You're safe now. It's over. No one's going to hurt you."

Molly's body slowly relaxed in Grim's arms, her anger draining away as the reality of what he was saying began to sink in. For the first time in days—perhaps even weeks—she felt the overwhelming weight of exhaustion wash over her. Her head lolled against Grim's chest, her breath still coming in shallow, ragged bursts, but the fight had left her.

"I... I didn't think I'd ever get out," Molly whispered, her voice broken with emotion. "I thought... I thought she'd win."

Grim tightened his grip on her, his voice soft but firm. "You're safe now, Molly. She's not going to hurt you anymore."

Across the room, Clo approached DarkSeraphim cautiously. The woman lay crumpled on the bed, her face twisted in pain and covered and blood and scratch marks; she clutched her back where the broken springs had cut deep into her skin. Blood was seeping through her shirt, but Clo could see that DarkSeraphim's injuries were more than just physical. The woman's eyes were wide, filled with something Clo had never expected to see—fear.

For the first time, DarkSeraphim was truly afraid. She knew it was over. There would be no more slipping away, no more running, no more manipulating. Molly had fought back, and now the police were here. There was no escape this time.

Clo pulled out her radio, her voice steady as she called for backup. "Control, this is Sergeant Harper. We need immediate backup and medical assistance. The suspect is in custody, victim recovered. Location confirmed—repeat, location confirmed."

The voice on the other end crackled with acknowledgement. "Copy that, Sergeant. Backup and ambulance en route. ETA ten minutes."

Clo lowered the radio and turned her gaze back to DarkSeraphim, her eyes narrowing with a mixture of relief and disgust. This was the woman who had caused so much pain, so much suffering—yet here she was, crumpled on a bed, defeated.

DarkSeraphim's eyes flickered up to meet Clo's, filled with pain and fear. She knew what was coming. The sirens were growing louder in the distance, their wail piercing the otherwise quiet night. Her time was up.

But even as she lay there, clutching her bleeding back, a small part of DarkSeraphim's mind was already planning. *I won't stay locked up. I'll get out. I'll find a way.* Her nails dug into her palms as she clenched her fists, her jaw set with silent resolve. *This isn't the end for me.*

Clo crouched down beside her, her voice cold and final. "It's over," she said quietly. "You won't hurt anyone else."

DarkSeraphim didn't reply. She just stared at the ceiling, her mind already working on her next move. It wasn't over. Not for her. There was always a way out, and she would find it.

As Grim continued to hold Molly, he felt her body finally relax completely in his arms. The adrenaline had worn off, leaving only exhaustion in its place. Her head rested against his chest, and he could feel her trembling slightly, her breath coming in soft, shaky bursts.

She had survived. The nightmare was over. She was going home.

Grim glanced over at Clo, who was keeping a close eye on DarkSeraphim. The relief was palpable in the room now—relief that Molly was alive, that DarkSeraphim was finally caught, that this nightmare was coming to an end.

But despite the relief, Grimshaw couldn't shake the feeling that something was still unresolved. DarkSeraphim was just one piece of the puzzle. There were still so many unanswered questions and so many loose threads that needed to be tied up.

But for now, Molly was safe. And that was what mattered.

Chapter 31: The Aftermath

The flashing blue and red lights of the police cars reflected off the shattered windows of the old farmhouse, casting long shadows across the overgrown yard. The sound of footsteps crunching against the gravel echoed in the night as paramedics and officers swarmed the scene, voices urgent but hushed, the tension thick in the air. Grimshaw stood outside, leaning against the side of the car, his mind still reeling from the chaotic events that had just unfolded.

Molly was safe. That thought grounded him, even as the weight of everything else threatened to crush him. He had spent so long chasing shadows, wondering if Molly would be another face he failed to save. But she wasn't. Molly had survived.

Grimshaw exhaled slowly, his breath forming clouds in the cold night air. Across the yard, he could see Molly sitting in the back of an ambulance, wrapped in a thick blanket. She was staring ahead, her eyes distant, her body slumped with exhaustion. She hadn't spoken since they had pulled her away from DarkSeraphim. There were no more screams, no more wild, desperate fights—just silence.

Clo stood beside her, one hand gently resting on Molly's shoulder, talking to the paramedics. Every now and then, she would glance back toward Grimshaw, her eyes reflecting the same exhaustion he felt.

As Grim watched Molly, his chest tightened. He knew this moment wasn't the end—it was the beginning of a long road. Molly was alive, but the girl who had walked out of that farmhouse wasn't the same one who had been taken. She had fought her captor with a ferocity he hadn't expected, but now that the battle was over, the toll it had taken on her was evident in every movement, every hollow expression.

Inside the ambulance, Molly sat on the edge of the gurney, her legs dangling off the side, staring at the ground as if it were the only thing anchoring her. The thick blanket around her shoulders felt heavy, but it didn't offer any real warmth. She couldn't feel it. Everything around her felt distant, muffled as if she were trapped inside a glass box, watching the world from a distance.

"Molly, sweetheart, can you hear me?" Clo's voice pierced through the fog, soft but steady.

Molly blinked, her gaze slowly lifting to meet Clo's. The Sargent's face was kind, her eyes filled with a mix of concern and something else, admiration, maybe? But Molly couldn't process that. She felt... nothing.

"I know you've been through something unimaginable," Clo continued, crouching down to meet Molly's eye level. "But you're safe now. We're here for you, okay?"

Safe…….The word echoed in Molly's mind, bouncing around as if it were some foreign concept she didn't understand. Could she ever feel safe again? After everything that had happened—after everything she had done—how could she ever go back to normal?

Her hands tightened into fists beneath the blanket, her nails digging into her palms. She didn't feel safe. She didn't feel anything. The anger, the fury that had driven her to fight back against DarkSeraphim, had drained out of her, leaving behind a hollow shell. What had it all been for? What had it cost her?

"Your parents are on their way," Clo said gently, her hand still resting on Molly's shoulder. "They'll be here soon."

Molly's heart clenched painfully at the mention of her parents. Mom... Dad. She hadn't seen them in what felt like an eternity. The thought of facing them now, after everything, made her chest tighten with guilt. How could she look them in the eye after what had happened? How could she explain what she had been through—what she had become?

Tears stung her eyes, but she blinked them back. She couldn't cry. Not now. Not in front of all these people. She had to hold it together, even if everything inside her was crumbling.

Across the yard, officers led DarkSeraphim out of the farmhouse, her wrists bound tightly behind her back. Blood still stained her shirt from the scratches Molly had left on her face and arms. Despite her physical injuries, DarkSeraphim's expression was cold and emotionless. There was no sign of fear, no regret—just the hollow calm of a woman who had calculated every move, even as the world collapsed around her.

She kept her head held high as she was escorted to the waiting police car, her eyes scanning the scene with a sense of detachment. The handcuffs bit into her skin, but she didn't flinch. The sirens wailed, echoing in the distance, but she barely heard them. Her mind was elsewhere—already planning her next move.

As DarkSeraphim was placed in the back of the car, she caught Grimshaw's gaze. For a brief moment, their eyes locked, and a cold smile tugged at the corner of her mouth. It was a smile that sent a chill down Grimshaw's spine—a silent message that said, this isn't over.

Grimshaw's jaw tightened, his fists clenching at his sides. He knew what that look meant. DarkSeraphim wasn't broken. She was waiting. Waiting for her chance to escape, to rebuild, to continue her work, and that terrified him more than anything else.

But not tonight. Tonight, she was going to jail.

As the police car drove away, Grimshaw stood there, staring after it, his mind heavy with the weight of everything that had just happened. The sense of victory he had expected to feel was absent. There was no triumph in this. The only relief that Molly had survived—and the bitter knowledge that this case wasn't truly over.

He had spent years chasing DarkSeraphim, always one step behind, always just missing her. Tonight, he had caught her, but it didn't feel like a win. Not yet. There were too many loose ends, too many unanswered questions. DarkSeraphim had been a ghost for years, operating in the shadows, weaving a web of manipulation and deceit and yes now that they had her in custody, Grimshaw knew there was still much more to unravel.

He glanced back at Molly, watching as she sat silently in the ambulance, staring down at her clenched hands. She was safe, but he could see the toll the ordeal had taken on her. She wasn't the same girl who had disappeared only a couple of days ago, That much was clear.

Clo approached him, her face lined with exhaustion. "Backup's here. They'll be handling the scene, processing everything."

Grimshaw nodded, his eyes still on Molly. "She's going to need a lot of support."

"Yeah," Clo agreed, following his gaze. "But she's a fighter. She'll get through this."

Grimshaw remained silent for a moment, lost in thought. Finally, he spoke. "We caught DarkSeraphim, but it's not over."

Clo raised an eyebrow, her expression hardening. "You think she's part of something bigger?"

"I know she is," Grimshaw replied, his voice grim. "There's a whole network behind her. We've barely scratched the surface. DarkSeraphim's just one piece of the puzzle."

Clo sighed, rubbing the back of her neck. "Then we've got a long road ahead of us."

Grimshaw nodded, his jaw set with determination. "Yeah. But we'll finish it. We owe Molly that much."

The sound of a car pulling up broke the heavy silence that had settled over the farmyard. Molly's head jerked up, her heart pounding as she saw her parents rush out of the vehicle, their faces etched with worry and relief. Amanda reached her first, pulling her into a tight, trembling embrace, tears streaming down her face.

"Molly, my baby," Amanda whispered, her voice choked with emotion. "Thank God you're safe."

Molly felt her mother's arms around her, felt the warmth and love, but she couldn't bring herself to respond. She was numb. She didn't know how to feel or what to say. The warmth of the embrace clashed with the cold emptiness inside her, and all she could do was sit there, silent, as her mother cried into her shoulder.

Paul stood a few feet away, his face pale and drawn. His eyes were red from crying, but he didn't move to embrace Molly. He just stood there, watching, guilt and shame weighing heavily on him. He knew what he had done—what his actions had cost his family and he knew that no number of apologies could make up for it.

Molly glanced at him briefly, her eyes meeting his for a fraction of a second. But she quickly looked away, her heart aching. She wasn't ready to face him—not yet. There was too much between them, too much left unsaid.

"I'm so sorry, Molly," Paul whispered, his voice barely audible.

Molly didn't respond. She couldn't, not yet.

Chapter 32: The Web Unravels

The fluorescent lights buzzed quietly in the interrogation room, casting a sterile glow over the metal table. DarkSeraphim sat at its centre, her wrists bound by handcuffs, but her posture was unnervingly calm. Her sharp eyes flitted between Grimshaw and Clo, a cold, calculated smirk playing at the edges of her lips. She had been stripped of her false identities, her layers of manipulation peeled back, but she still carried the air of someone who believed she held the upper hand.

Grimshaw leaned against the wall, arms crossed, his eyes never leaving her. Clo sat across from DarkSeraphim, the tension in the room thick, ready to snap. They had finally caught her—DarkSeraphim, the woman who had haunted their nightmares and destroyed countless lives and yet, as Clo looked into the eyes of this criminal mastermind, she couldn't help but feel that they were still a step behind.

DarkSeraphim broke the silence first, her voice dripping with false sympathy. "You look tired, Sarge͡nt. You should rest. This game takes a toll, doesn't it?"

Clo ignored the bait, her face impassive. "We're not here to play games. You're facing multiple counts of trafficking, kidnapping, and assault. You can spend the rest of your life in prison, or you can start talking now and make this easier for yourself."

DarkSeraphim's smirk deepened, her eyes flicking to Grimshaw, who hadn't moved. "Ah, Detective Grimshaw. Still so quiet. I expected more from you. After all, we've danced this dance before, haven't we?"

Grimshaw's jaw tightened, but he didn't respond. He had learned long ago not to engage with her provocations. She thrived on manipulation, on getting under your skin. Every word out of her mouth was a move in a larger game—a game Grimshaw was determined not to lose.

Clo continued, her tone sharp. "We've got enough evidence to put you away for life, so don't think you're walking out of here. The question is whether you want to spend that life rotting in a maximum-security prison or if you want to help yourself by cooperating."

DarkSeraphim's eyes flickered with amusement. She leaned back in her chair, crossing her legs casually. "Cooperate? And what would that entail, exactly? Telling you all about my little operation?" She tilted her head, her voice mocking. "You're smart, Detective Clo. Surely you've figured out most of it by now."

Grimshaw leaned forward, his voice cold. "We know you're not working alone. You've got contacts, accomplices—people who've helped you traffic girls across borders. We want names. Locations. Details of the ring you're a part of."

DarkSeraphim's expression shifted ever so slightly—a flicker of something that resembled pride. "You think this is all about me? You really have no idea how deep this goes, do you?"

Clo leaned forward, her voice low but firm. "Enlighten us."

DarkSeraphim smiled—a slow, predatory grin. "You've barely scratched the surface. I'm just one piece of a much larger network. The trafficking ring you're chasing spans countries and continents. It's not something you can dismantle by locking me up. There are others out there—more dangerous than you can imagine."

Grimshaw's hands clenched into fists at his sides. He had always suspected that DarkSeraphim was part of a larger operation but hearing it from her lips made the reality even grimmer. This wasn't just about Molly—it was about hundreds, maybe thousands, of victims. The web was far-reaching, and cutting off the head wouldn't destroy the body.

"You can't win," DarkSeraphim continued, her voice dripping with satisfaction. "Even if you stop me, there are others ready to take my place. It's been going on for decades, Detective. You think a couple of arrests will change that?"

Clo remained unfazed, though Grimshaw could feel the tension radiating from her. "You still have a choice," she said evenly. "You can give us names—locations. Help us dismantle the network. Or you can rot in a cell knowing we'll take them down without you."

DarkSeraphim chuckled softly, shaking her head. "You still don't get it. You'll never take them down and even if you do chip away, there's always someone else ready to step in. You're fighting a losing battle."

Grimshaw had heard enough. He slammed his hand down on the table, his voice icy. "Where's Lisa Stewart? How deep is she involved?"

For the first time, DarkSeraphim's expression shifted. The mention of Lisa's name elicited a subtle change—her smirk faltered, and her eyes flickered with something that resembled uncertainty. It was brief, but Grimshaw caught it. *So, there it is*, he thought. *She's afraid of something.*

"Lisa?" DarkSeraphim repeated, her voice soft but tinged with bitterness. "Lisa was... useful. But she was never the one pulling the strings. She thought she was in control, but in the end, she was just another pawn."

Clo narrowed her eyes. "A pawn in whose game?"

DarkSeraphim's lips pressed into a thin line. She said nothing for a moment, her eyes narrowing in thought. Grimshaw leaned in, his voice low and dangerous. "Tell us who's pulling the strings. You give us a name, and maybe we'll consider leniency."

DarkSeraphim's eyes flicked to him, calculating. For a moment, she seemed to consider it, the wheels in her mind turning as she weighed her options. But then, just as quickly, she seemed to make up her mind. She leaned back in her chair, crossing her arms, her smirk returning.

"Nice try, Detective Grimshaw," she purred, her voice full of mockery. "But I think I'll keep that little secret to myself."

Grimshaw's jaw clenched, but Clo intervened before he could push further. She knew that getting emotional with DarkSeraphim wouldn't help their case. This woman thrived on psychological warfare, and they couldn't afford to play into her hands.

"That's fine," Clo said coolly, standing up from the table. "You can stay silent. It doesn't matter. We'll tear your network apart piece by piece, starting with Lisa."

DarkSeraphim's smirk wavered, but she said nothing. She watched as Clo and Grimshaw turned to leave the room, her eyes burning with silent defiance. She knew they were closing in, but she wouldn't make it easy for them.

As they stepped out of the interrogation room, Grimshaw let out a sharp breath, his frustration boiling over. "She's not going to give us anything. She'd rather see her empire burn than admit defeat."

Clo nodded, her expression grim. "But we don't need her to talk. We've got enough evidence to put her away but the bigger fish has to be Lisa Stewart, but once we get her in custody, the rest of the operation will start to unravel."

Grimshaw's mind was already racing, thinking ahead. Lisa Stewart was their next target, and she was the key to unlocking the deeper levels of the trafficking ring. DarkSeraphim may have been the face of the operation, but Lisa had connections they needed to expose and if they could get to Lisa, they could start tearing the web apart from the inside.

Clo glanced at Grimshaw, her voice softening slightly. "We'll get them, Grim. This isn't over."

Grimshaw nodded, but the weight of the case still pressed heavily on his shoulders. DarkSeraphim was just one piece of a much larger puzzle, and the deeper they dug, the darker the picture became. He knew this wasn't just about Molly anymore—this was about stopping an entire network of traffickers who preyed on the vulnerable, the lost, the forgotten.

As they made their way back to the incident room, Grimshaw's phone buzzed. It was Samantha, calling from Houghton-le-Spring. "Grimshaw, it's urgent. We've got evidence linking Lisa Stewart directly to the trafficking operation. I'm heading there now with a team to bring her in."

Grimshaw's heart raced. This was the breakthrough they needed.

"Good," he said, his voice hard with determination. "Make sure she doesn't slip away."

Chapter 33: Lisa's Denial

The sky had darkened into a heavy slate grey as Grimshaw and Clo pulled up outside Lisa Stewart's suburban home. The street was eerily quiet as if the entire neighbourhood sensed the storm that was about to break. A row of neatly kept gardens and identical houses lined the street, each one standing like a silent witness to what was about to unfold. But inside that seemingly ordinary house, Lisa Stewart was hiding a secret that could shatter everything Molly's family thought they knew.

Grimshaw cut the engine, his hand gripping the steering wheel for a moment before exhaling. He exchanged a look with Clo. They both knew this was a critical moment. Lisa wasn't just a side player in this trafficking ring—she had been embedded in Molly's life, close to her family, and manipulating Paul for months. Her betrayal would shake the Reid family to its core.

"She won't go down without a fight," Clo muttered, her eyes hard as she unbuckled her seatbelt.

"She's been in control for too long," Grimshaw replied. "People like Lisa don't give up control easily."

They stepped out of the car, the cold evening air biting at their faces as they approached the front door. Grimshaw glanced at the other unmarked cars parked along the street—backup was ready. They couldn't afford to lose Lisa. If she slipped away, the entire case could unravel.

Clo knocked on the door, her fist hitting the wood with a sharp, authoritative rap. They waited, the silence pressing down on them as the moments stretched out. Grimshaw's heart thudded in his chest, his mind racing with the possibilities. Would Lisa run? Would she fight? He wasn't sure, but he knew they had to be ready for anything.

After what felt like an eternity, the door opened, and Lisa Stewart stood before them. Her expression was calm, her face carefully composed, but there was a flicker of recognition—of calculation—in her eyes when she saw Grimshaw and Clo standing on her doorstep.

"Officers," she greeted, her voice smooth, almost friendly. "To what do I owe the pleasure?"

Grimshaw felt a surge of anger rise inside him, but he pushed it down. Lisa was trying to keep control of the situation, to maintain her facade of normality. But they were here to tear it down.

"We need to talk, Mrs Stewart," Grimshaw said, his voice steady but cold. "May we come in?"

Lisa's eyes flickered briefly to the side as if she were considering her options. But then, with a gracious smile that didn't reach her eyes, she stepped aside and gestured for them to enter. "Of course."

As they crossed the threshold into her pristine living room, Grimshaw couldn't help but feel the eerie contrast between the normalcy of Lisa's home and the darkness of what she was involved in. The room was immaculate—tasteful furniture, framed photos of Lisa doing different activities, climbing, skiing, kayaking and bookshelves lined with novels. It was a world away from the chaos and suffering she had caused.

Clo closed the door behind them, her eyes sharp as she scanned the room. "We know about your involvement with DarkSeraphim," she said bluntly, her voice cutting through the false pleasantries.

Lisa's composure faltered for a split second, but she recovered quickly, her smile tightening. "I'm not sure what you're talking about. Dark who?"

"You know exactly who we are talking about, the trafficking ring you are involved in, we know it is you that has been in charge," said Grim,

"Sorry doesn't ring a bell" smiled Lisa,

"Ah, my apologies I just need to make a quick call" Grim removed his phone as he said this and he flicked through the contacts until he reached the number he had taken from the phone removed from DarkSeraphim that had been the main contact on their device. He hit the call button and lifted the phone to his ear.

Suddenly a ringing came from one of the drawers in the unit standing in the corner of the room, "Your sideboard appears to be ringing, would you like a moment to answer it?" Clo asked her voice staying calm,

Lisa's eyes flicked to the sideboard and then to the patio doors at the back of the room, "don't think about running we have your home surrounded" said Grim and he moved over and opened the drawer to find the burner phone. As he pressed the end call the burner phone stopped ringing.

Grimshaw stepped forward, his eyes locking onto hers. "We've got evidence, Lisa. Text messages, financial records—everything that links you to the trafficking ring and I bet there is more information on this" he said as he held the device in front of her, "This isn't just about blackmailing Paul anymore. You are part of something much bigger, and it's time you started talking."

The mask slipped. Lisa's eyes darkened, and the charm she had so carefully cultivated vanished. She crossed her arms, her posture stiffening as she dropped the pretence. "You have no idea what you're dealing with," she hissed, her voice cold. "You think you can just waltz in here and make me confess? You're way out of your depth."

Clo didn't flinch. "Maybe. But we're here, and we've got enough to bring you in. So, you can either talk to us now, or we can do this at the station."

Lisa's eyes flicked between them, her mind clearly racing. For the first time, Grimshaw saw the cracks in her composure, the fear creeping in behind the bravado. She was cornered, and she knew it.

"You think you're so clever," Lisa sneered, her voice dripping with contempt. "You think you've figured it all out. But you're just playing into their hands. You're not even close to understanding the scope of this operation."

Grimshaw's jaw clenched. "Enlighten us."

Lisa's gaze hardened. "You think DarkSeraphim is the mastermind? She's nothing but a puppet. The real power behind this network—the ones pulling the strings—they're untouchable. You can arrest me, arrest DarkSeraphim, but it won't stop anything. There are others—smarter, more dangerous than you can imagine."

Clo's eyes narrowed. "We've heard that before. But you're still part of it, and you're still going down."

Lisa let out a bitter laugh. "You're so naïve. Do you think taking me down will solve everything? It won't. I'm just one piece of the puzzle. The people I work for—people like DarkSeraphim—they're connected. They've been doing this for decades. You can't touch them."

Grimshaw took a step closer, his voice low but filled with conviction. "We don't need to bring down the whole operation today. We just need to bring down enough of it to save Molly—and the others like her and it starts with you."

Lisa's eyes flared with something close to fury. "Molly," she spat, her voice thick with disdain. "She was never supposed to be involved. She was collateral damage, thanks to Paul's incompetence. If he hadn't been so weak, none of this would have happened."

Grimshaw's hands tightened into fists. "You manipulated him. You blackmailed him. And then you used his daughter as leverage when he couldn't pay. Don't try to pin all of this on him."

Lisa's lip curled in a sneer. "You have no idea what it takes to survive in this world. Paul was weak, pathetic—an easy target. He deserved everything he got."

"And Molly, did she deserve any of this?" Clo shot back, her voice sharp.

Lisa's expression flickered with something—guilt, perhaps, but it was gone as quickly as it had appeared. She straightened, her voice steady once more. "I've done what I had to do to survive. You think I'm the villain here, but you don't know half of what goes on in this world. People like me... we're survivors. We do what we have to."

Grimshaw felt a surge of disgust rise inside him. He had heard this kind of justification before—this twisted logic that was supposed to turn predators into victims. But Lisa was no victim. She had chosen this path, and she had dragged innocent people down with her.

"You can justify it all you want," Grimshaw said coldly. "But you're still going to prison."

Before Lisa could respond, the sound of footsteps echoed from the front door. Two uniformed officers entered the room, their faces grim. "Mrs. Stewart, you're under arrest," one of them said, stepping forward with handcuffs.

Lisa's face tightened, but she didn't resist. As they cuffed her hands behind her back, she turned to Grimshaw one last time, her eyes burning with hatred. "This won't end with me. You'll see. This network—these people—they're untouchable."

Grimshaw said nothing as they led her out of the house, her words hanging in the air like a dark cloud. Clo stood beside him, her expression hard. They had won a battle, but the war was far from over. DarkSeraphim's network was vast, and Lisa had just confirmed their worst fear—there were more players out there, hidden in the shadows, waiting to take her place.

"She's right," Clo said quietly. "This isn't over."

Grimshaw nodded, his mind already turning to the next steps. "But we've got her," he replied. "And that's a start."

As the officers escorted Lisa to the waiting patrol car, Grimshaw and Clo stood in the quiet of the now-empty house. The scent of Lisa's expensive perfume still lingered in the air, a reminder of the twisted duplicity they had just unravelled.

Chapter 34: DarkSeraphim's Endgame

The heavy clank of the cell door reverberated through the small, dimly lit detention block as it slammed shut behind DarkSeraphim. The chill of the concrete walls pressed in on her from all sides, the harsh fluorescent light above casting cold shadows on her face. DarkSeraphim sat on the thin cot, her hands resting on her lap, her posture unnervingly calm despite the iron bars that now separated her from the outside world.

The capture had been a setback, but it wasn't the end. DarkSeraphim had always planned for contingencies. She knew that one day the law would catch up to her. But she had never planned on staying locked up. She still had her contacts, her network, and the reach of her empire. Even in this small cell, she felt a flicker of control. She wasn't out of moves yet.

She shifted slightly, her mind calculating, always calculating. She had to wait for the right moment, the right opportunity to escape. And when it came, she would be ready.

Grimshaw sat at his desk in the Washington police station, sifting through a mountain of paperwork related to DarkSeraphim's arrest and the growing trafficking case. The room was silent, save for the steady hum of the computers and the occasional ring of phones. He had been reviewing statements, building the case against her, but something gnawed at the back of his mind—something he couldn't shake.

DarkSeraphim had been too calm during her interrogation. Her smugness had been infuriating, but it was also telling. She had practically taunted them with the knowledge that the trafficking ring wasn't just about her—that it went deeper, wider than they could imagine. She seemed confident, even as the handcuffs had tightened around her wrists. Grimshaw had seen criminals try to bluff their way out of situations before, but DarkSeraphim was different. She wasn't bluffing.

"She's planning something," Grimshaw muttered to himself, flipping through the interrogation notes. His instincts were rarely wrong. He had felt it before, that eerie certainty that something wasn't right. And now that feeling had returned, stronger than ever.

Just as the thought crossed his mind, his phone buzzed, interrupting the quiet. It was Sergeant Clo.

"Grim, we've got a problem," Clo's voice was clipped, tense. "I've just received word from Durham Control. There's chatter about a possible escape attempt. Some of DarkSeraphim's contacts are moving."

Grimshaw's stomach dropped. "Escape?" he repeated, his grip tightening on the phone. "She's locked up at the secure unit. How could she possibly—"

"They're saying it's coordinated. Internal help," Clo cut in. "Her people are trying to break her out. We need to move now!"

Grimshaw was already on his feet, grabbing his jacket. "Where is she being held?"

"HM Prison Low Newton. I've already called for backup, but we need to get there before anything happens."

"I'm on my way," Grimshaw said, ending the call and bolting from the station.

Inside the high-security prison, DarkSeraphim sat in her cell, her calm demeanour unchanged despite the growing tension outside. She could feel it in the air—the shift, the movement. Her people were coming. She had made the necessary arrangements long before her arrest, knowing that if it ever came to this, she wouldn't be alone. The web she had spun extended far beyond these walls, and her loyalists were ready to act.

The guards at the facility had no idea that an external threat was brewing. DarkSeraphim's operation had always been subtle, and precise. But now, the plan was already in motion. On the outside, her associates—members of the trafficking ring who owed their freedom to her—were making their move. Disguised as maintenance workers, they had slipped into the secure perimeter of the facility, waiting for the right moment to strike.

DarkSeraphim knew her time was limited. She had to be ready when the signal came.

As the clock approached midnight, a series of alarms suddenly blared through the halls of the remand centre. Chaos erupted as guards rushed to contain what appeared to be a breach in the facility's main gate. The so-called "maintenance workers" had detonated a small, controlled explosion, shattered the security protocols and allowed a small team of armed men to infiltrate the building. It was the distraction they needed to draw attention away from DarkSeraphim's cell.

Inside, DarkSeraphim stood calmly, waiting. She had been briefed on the plan, and everything was unfolding exactly as she had envisioned. The guards were panicking, scrambling to secure the entrance, while the real threat was moving silently through the lower levels of the building, closing in on her.

She heard the familiar click of footsteps approaching her cell door. Her heart quickened, but she kept her composure. This was her moment.

Grimshaw and Clo arrived at the remand centre just as the chaos was unfolding. Flashing blue lights bathed the facility in a cold, urgent glow, and the sound of alarms filled the night air. Armed officers were swarming the area, trying to control the situation, but the scene was already spiralling out of control.

"We need to get inside!" Grimshaw barked at one of the officers posted near the entrance. "DarkSeraphim is the target. They're trying to break her out."

The officer nodded, waving them through. "We've locked down the perimeter, but there's been a breach. We're trying to contain it."

Grimshaw and Clo pushed their way inside, adrenaline surging through their veins. They had to stop this. If DarkSeraphim escaped now, they would lose everything.

As they rushed through the halls, Grimshaw's mind raced. He couldn't let her slip away—not after everything. He thought of Molly, of all the victims, still out there, trapped in the web of this trafficking ring. DarkSeraphim had to face justice.

They reached the cell block just as the power flickered. Clo cursed under her breath. "She's getting out. I know it."

Grimshaw's heart pounded in his chest. "Not if we stop her."

DarkSeraphim's cell door creaked open, and two masked men stepped inside. They were quick and efficient—one of them handed DarkSeraphim a small set of clothes and a gun. She didn't speak, merely nodding in acknowledgement as she changed out of her prison uniform.

But as she moved toward the door, her escape now just within reach, a voice called out behind her.

"Going somewhere?"

DarkSeraphim froze, her pulse spiking. She turned slowly, her eyes narrowing as she saw Grimshaw and Clo standing at the end of the corridor, guns drawn. Grimshaw's expression was hard, determined. He wasn't going to let her walk out of there.

The two masked men raised their weapons, "Drop the weapons!" Clo barked, her voice cutting through the chaos.

For a moment, everything hung in the balance. DarkSeraphim's eyes flicked between her would-be rescuers and the officers blocking her exit. She had come too far to be stopped now.

With a sudden, sharp movement, she raised her gun and aimed it directly at Grimshaw. "You can't stop me!" she hissed, her voice filled with venom.

But before she could pull the trigger, Grimshaw fired first. The shot rang out, loud and final. DarkSeraphim's body jerked backwards as the bullet struck her shoulder, her gun clattering to the floor as she stumbled.

The masked men hesitated for a split second—just long enough for Clo to move in, disarming them and forcing them to the ground. The guards, alerted by the commotion, rushed in to secure the area, handcuffing the men and dragging them away.

DarkSeraphim lay on the cold floor, clutching her bleeding shoulder, her face twisted in pain. Grimshaw approached cautiously, his gun still trained on her, but there was no fight left in her now. Her escape attempt had failed.

"It's over," Grimshaw said, his voice cold as he stood over her.

DarkSeraphim's lips curled into a bitter smile, even as the pain coursed through her. "Is it? You'll never take down the whole network. There's always someone else. Always."

Grimshaw didn't respond. He knew she was right, to an extent. There would always be others. But today, they had taken down one of the most dangerous predators he had ever faced, and no matter how small it was, it was still a victory.

Clo knelt beside DarkSeraphim, applying pressure to the wound. "You're going to rot in prison for the rest of your life," she said quietly. "You'll never hurt anyone again."

DarkSeraphim's eyes fluttered shut, her breath coming in shallow, ragged gasps. "We'll see," she whispered, the fight finally leaving her.

As the paramedics arrived to take DarkSeraphim away, Grimshaw holstered his gun and let out a long, slow breath. The chase was over.

For now.

Chapter 35: Healing and Moving Forward

The hospital room was quiet, the sterile smell of disinfectant mixing with the soft hum of machinery monitoring Molly's vitals. Sunlight streamed in through the tall windows, bathing the room in a gentle warmth, a stark contrast to the chaos Molly had escaped just days before. She lay still in the hospital bed, her face pale, her eyes closed in uneasy sleep. Her chest rose and fell in shallow, steady breaths.

Amanda sat by her daughter's bedside, her hands folded in her lap, her eyes fixed on Molly's face. The past few days had been a whirlwind of emotions—fear, relief, anger, and overwhelming sorrow all crashing down on her in waves. Her daughter was back, but the girl lying in the hospital bed was not the same Molly who had disappeared. She was haunted, bruised not just in body but in spirit, and Amanda couldn't help but feel that a piece of Molly had been lost forever.

The sound of the door creaking open broke Amanda from her thoughts. She turned to see Paul standing hesitantly in the doorway, his face drawn and haggard. He had been by Molly's side too, but always at a distance, unsure of his place, unsure of how to be the father he hadn't been during the months leading up to Molly's disappearance.

Amanda's chest tightened. The betrayal still stung—Paul's affair, his lies, the blackmail that had put Molly in danger. But now, with Molly lying there, fragile and recovering, everything seemed muddled. The anger she felt toward Paul warred with her exhaustion, her need to focus on Molly, her desire to rebuild their family.

Paul took a tentative step inside, his eyes filled with guilt and pain. "How…..how is she?" he asked softly, his voice barely above a whisper.

Amanda didn't answer right away. Her gaze drifted back to Molly, her heart heavy with the weight of everything unsaid between her and Paul. The silence stretched, thick with unspoken words.

"She's... resting," Amanda finally said, her voice quiet but steady. "The doctors say she's stable, but she's been through so much. They're not sure how long it will take for her to process everything."

Paul nodded, his eyes never leaving Molly. He moved closer, standing awkwardly at the foot of the bed. "I want to help her," he said, his voice cracking. "I know I can't undo what happened, but I need to be there for her now. I can't lose her, Amanda. I can't."

Amanda's grip tightened on the edge of the hospital bed. Her emotions swirled in a confusing mess. She wanted to scream at Paul, to blame him for everything, but she was also too exhausted for anger. All she wanted was for Molly to be safe, to heal, and maybe—just maybe—for their family to find a way back to each other.

"I don't know if we can ever go back to what we were," Amanda whispered, her eyes glistening with unshed tears. "Too much has happened."

Paul swallowed hard; guilt etched deeply into his features. "I know, and, and I'm so sorry. I don't expect forgiveness... but I can't give up on her. Or on us."

The silence between them felt heavy, but the weight of it wasn't as crushing as it had been before. They both stood in the same space now united in their concern for Molly, but separated by the distance of the betrayal.

Amanda sighed softly. "Right now, all we can do is focus on Molly. We need to help her heal. The rest? Well we will see, you will have to tell her everything, she needs to know especially if the police take it further about your involvement, but for now, her recovery is the main thing"

Paul nodded, his voice barely a whisper. "Yeah. We do."

As the days passed, Molly slowly began to emerge from the fog of her trauma. The bruises on her body began to fade, but the emotional scars remained raw, invisible but ever-present. She had been through a nightmare—one that no one her age should ever have to endure—and now, with the immediate danger behind her, she was left to confront the memories that haunted her.

Molly was quiet most of the time, her voice barely above a whisper when she did speak. She avoided eye contact, her gaze often distant, lost in thoughts she couldn't fully express. The doctors had suggested therapy, a long road to recovery, but Molly wasn't sure if she was ready to open up. How could she explain what she had gone through? How could anyone understand the fear, the isolation, the betrayal she had felt?

But Molly wasn't alone, Amanda was there, every day, sitting by her bedside, gently encouraging her to talk, to let out the storm that had been brewing inside her and slowly—painfully—Molly began to share pieces of what she had been through. The terror,....The lies DarkSeraphim had fed her. The suffocating sense that no one could save her.

"There were times when, when I didn't think I'd ever come home," Molly whispered one afternoon, her voice breaking as tears welled in her eyes. "I thought... I thought I'd never see you again."

Amanda reached out, squeezing Molly's hand gently. "You're safe now, Molly. We're going to get through this. Together."

Molly nodded, but the weight of her trauma still pressed down on her. Healing would take time—maybe years. But with her mother's support, she felt a flicker of hope that one day, she could move beyond the darkness.

Grimshaw sat alone in his office, the dim light from the window casting long shadows across his desk. The case file on DarkSeraphim lay open in front of him, filled with notes, photographs, and evidence that spanned months of investigation since the arrest. It was over—at least this part of it. DarkSeraphim had been moved to an isolation unit, Lisa Stewart was also locked up, and the immediate threat to Molly had been neutralised. But the victory felt hollow.

The trafficking ring DarkSeraphim had been a part of was larger than they had imagined, and while one piece of the network had been dismantled, Grimshaw knew that many others still operated in the shadows. He had seen this before. Cutting off one head of the hydra didn't kill the beast. There were always others ready to take its place.

His mind wandered to Molly. She had been the catalyst for this case, the reason Grimshaw had become so personally invested. The thought of her, trapped in that world, had fuelled him, driven him to push harder, to dig deeper, and now she was safe. But the case had taken its toll—on her, on her family, and on him.

Grimshaw leaned back in his chair, running a hand through his hair. The face of the girl he had failed in Cornwall flashed in his mind. He had promised himself that Molly's case wouldn't end the same way— that he wouldn't let her slip through his fingers like the last one and he hadn't. But it didn't feel like redemption. It felt like survival.

A soft knock at the door pulled Grimshaw from his thoughts. Clo stepped in; her expression tired but satisfied. She glanced at the open case file on his desk before taking a seat across from him.

"How's Molly?" she asked, her voice gentle.

Grimshaw sighed. "She's recovering. Physically, at least. Emotionally... it's going to take time."

Clo nodded. "She's lucky to have her mam by her side." She looked at the files and said "Without your determination, who knows where she'd be now."

Grimshaw shook his head. "It wasn't just me. We got lucky. There are still so many out there, Clo. So many we didn't save."

Clo's eyes softened with understanding. "You can't save them all, Grim. But you saved Molly. You brought her home."

Grimshaw looked down at the file, the weight of the case pressing on him. "Yeah. We did."

Chapter 36: Epilogue – Justice Served

The courtroom was filled with an oppressive silence as DarkSeraphim stood before the judge, her hands bound in front of her, her expression cold and unyielding. The trial had been swift but exhaustive, a parade of evidence meticulously laid out before the jury: testimony from Grimshaw, Clo, and the survivors, forensic analysis from her devices and financial records that traced the depths of her trafficking operation. All of it painted a damning portrait of a woman who had preyed on the vulnerable, who had manipulated, exploited, and destroyed lives for profit and power.

Now, after months of hearings and testimonies, the moment had come for her sentencing. DarkSeraphim had been found guilty on all charges—human trafficking, kidnapping, blackmail, and a litany of other crimes too numerous to count and yet, as the judge prepared to deliver the final sentence, her face remained impassive, devoid of any regret or remorse.

Grimshaw and Clo sat in the back of the courtroom, their presence largely unnoticed amidst the sea of onlookers, reporters, and families of victims. It wasn't the first time they had seen a criminal like DarkSeraphim go to trial, but this felt different. For Grimshaw, it was personal.

"Stand for sentencing," the bailiff commanded, his voice echoing in the hushed room.

DarkSeraphim rose, her cuffs clinking softly as she [is she related?] did so, her gaze fixed firmly on the judge. She knew this wasn't the end for her. There were always ways to manipulate the system, to bide her time until her network could help her. At least, that's what she told herself.

The judge cleared his throat, his voice stern. "Katherine Reid, for the crimes of human trafficking, kidnapping, and conspiracy, this court finds you guilty on all counts. You are hereby sentenced to life imprisonment without the possibility of parole."

A murmur ran through the room, relief mixing with the tension that had filled the air for weeks. For the victims and their families, it was but a small victory. For Grimshaw and Clo, it was closure. But as Grimshaw watched Katherine being led away, her face a mask of cold indifference, he couldn't help but feel that this was just one battle in a much larger war.

"That's one down," Clo murmured from beside him, her voice low but steady. "But we both know there's more out there."

Grimshaw nodded, his eyes still on the door where DarkSeraphim had disappeared. "Yeah. There's always more."

Lisa Stewart had been sentenced a week earlier. Her trial had been quieter, with less media attention, but no less significant. Her betrayal of the Reid family and her involvement in the trafficking ring, had come as a shock to everyone who knew her. Her crimes—blackmail, fraud, and conspiracy—had earned her a long prison sentence, though not as severe as DarkSeraphim's. Lisa had tried to bargain, offering names and information in exchange for leniency, but her cooperation had come too late.

For Amanda and Molly, Lisa's sentencing had been both a relief and a final blow. The woman they had trusted, who had been so deeply embedded in their lives, was now revealed as a villain. The betrayal cut deep, and it would take time to heal from the emotional scars Lisa had left behind.

But justice had been served.

Grimshaw stood outside the courthouse, the crisp autumn air biting at his face as he watched the last of the reporters pack up and leave. The trial was over, this part of the case closed, and yet the weight of it still lingered in his mind. DarkSeraphim might be behind bars, but he knew better than to think the fight was over.

"Thinking of retirement yet?" Clo asked, stepping up beside him, her breath visible in the cold air.

Grimshaw chuckled, shaking his head. "You know me better than that."

Clo smiled, but it didn't reach her eyes. "This case was a big one. You should be proud."

Grimshaw shrugged, his gaze drifting across the street. "We stopped one element of the trafficking ring. But how many more are still out there? How many more girls are suffering right now because we haven't caught them yet?"

Clo sighed softly. "We'll never stop them all, Grim. But that doesn't mean we stop trying."

Grimshaw nodded the weight of her words sinking in. He had spent years chasing criminals like DarkSeraphim, and he knew there would always be more.

"I'm not done yet," Grimshaw said quietly, more to himself than to Clo. "Not until we find the rest of them."

Clo gave him a knowing look. "You never are. How about I treat you to a coffee?" and with a wink she added "A dark one"

Printed in Great Britain
by Amazon